X078830

D1137824

THE BO̲ ̲WHO MADE EVERYONE LAUGH is Helen's
first n̲ ̲ ̲l. She lives just outside Sheffield and has
worked̲ ̲ ̲n actress for many years. The idea for this
story ̲ ̲ ̲from her son, Lenny, who has a stammer:
she want̲ ̲ ̲ ̲write the book that he would love to read,
starring a child like him.

@HelenRutterUK

PRAISE FOR
THE BOY WHO MADE EVERYONE LAUGH

"Truly, a heart-tugger of a book. Between the jokes is an incredibly moving and uplifting portrayal of one boy's struggle to find his voice. In Billy Plimpton, Helen Rutter has created a wonderfully real and inspiring character who reminds us of the importance of kindness." **Jenny Pearson, bestselling author of** *The Miraculous Journey of Freddie Yates*

"This book is a great way of showing children how to be confident by having a sense of humour and making others laugh." **Baroness Floella Benjamin**

"Who can resist a bit of funny kindness? Not me!"
Liza Tarbuck

"A laugh out loud story, the like of which I've never read before." **Kerry Godliman**

"So funny and joyful." **Rachel Parris**

"This is the book that will make everyone laugh. Entertaining, endearing, emotional and brimming with empathy, it's like *Wonder* with one-liners."
Scott Evans, The Reader Teacher

THE BOY WHO MADE EVERYONE LAUGH

Helen Rutter

■SCHOLASTIC

Published in the UK by Scholastic Children's Books, 2021
Euston House, 24 Eversholt Street, London, NW1 1DB
A division of Scholastic Limited

London – New York – Toronto – Sydney – Auckland
Mexico City – New Delhi – Hong Kong

SCHOLASTIC and associated logos are trademarks and/or
registered trademarks of Scholastic Inc.

Text © Helen Rutter, 2021
Illustration © Andrew Bannecker, 2021

The right of Helen Rutter and Andrew Bannecker to be identified as
the author and illustrator of this work has been asserted by them.

ISBN 978 0702 30085 1

A CIP catalogue record for this book is available from the British Library.

All rights reserved.
This book is sold subject to the condition that it shall not, by way of trade or
otherwise, be lent, hired out or otherwise circulated in any form of binding
or cover other than that in which it is published. No part of this publication
may be reproduced, stored in a retrieval system, or transmitted in any form
or by any other means (electronic, mechanical, photocopying, recording or
otherwise) without prior written permission of Scholastic Limited.

Printed by Printed by CPI Group (UK) Ltd, Croydon, CR0 4YY
Papers used by Scholastic Children's Books are made
from wood grown in sustainable forests.

1 3 5 7 9 10 8 6 4 2

This is a work of fiction. Names, characters, places, incidents and dialogues
are products of the author's imagination or are used fictitiously. Any
resemblance to actual people, living or dead, events or locales is entirely
coincidental.

www.scholastic.co.uk

For Lenny and Cleo

CHAPTER 1

The past, the present and the future walked into a bar.
It was tense.

Everything I say is important. Or at least, that's what my mum tells me. Sometimes she makes me repeat it out loud. It's embarrassing. Saying anything out loud can be embarrassing when you're me.

That's what I'm doing right now. Practising. Over and over, in the mirror. You'll find me here pretty often; it's where I do most of my chatting. Watching my eyes tighten to a close and my jaw tense up.

"M-m-my name is B-B-B-Billy Pliiimpton a-a-a-and I have a stammer. My name is Billy Plimpton and I have a stammer. My naaame is Biiiiillly and I have a s-s-s-s-stammer."

If I *don't* stammer when I'm saying it, I go bright red. Like I'm lying to my own reflection. If I do get stuck then I still go red because stammering at yourself feels stupid. But my speech therapist once told me to practise. So I do. A LOT.

I only say this particular sentence on my own in my bedroom and never to real people. I wish I never had to explain that I've got something wrong with my speech. It helps, though, when new people have already been told, so that they aren't left trying to figure out what's going on with me. Some people take ages. It's hard to watch them trying to control their expression. So much going on in their eyes. Wondering if it's all just a joke. I wish it was.

That's the other thing I practise. Jokes. I LOVE jokes. Using words differently. Surprising people with a punchline. Laughing at my own reflection.

"W-w-w-w-what diiid the llama say when he got kiiiiiicked out of th-th-th-the zoo? Alpaca my b-b-b-baaaags!"

How can I be funny if I can't even speak? It's not easy to tell a joke when you can't get the words out. I ruin my own punchlines. It's very annoying. I spend hours watching comedians on YouTube.

How smoothly they speak; how fast. The delighted audience. I try desperately to copy them.

It's not always obvious that I have a stammer. Sometimes it just sounds like a big pause and other times like I'm singing one word for a really long time for no reason whatsoever. Like I'm having a competition with myself to see how long I can draw one word out. This afternoon I got stuck on the words "lemon drizzle" for what seemed like for ever. We were talking about our favourite cakes. The amount of time it took me to say it almost made me go off lemon drizzle cake a bit. Sometimes the words themselves annoy me, when I get stuck badly, like they are doing it on purpose.

My little sister Chloe's friend Aisha was over for tea today. They galloped around the kitchen making *clip-clop* sounds. Chloe's obsessed with ponies. Her room makes me feel sick, there are so many stuffed toy ponies everywhere and horse posters on the walls. I'm a bit scared of horses, but I would never tell her that. So I just don't go in there very often.

Aisha hadn't been to our house before. As we were eating our tea, I was singing my way through a new joke – "Wh-wh-wh-which hand is it better to write wiiiiith?" – when Aisha asked, "Why do you talk like that?" As blunt as that, looking right at me over her forkful of spaghetti.

So Chloe explained for me: "He gets stuck on his words. He knows what he wants to say but his brain won't let it come out properly. You just have to wait until he's finished."

Aisha thought about it for a while, then sucked up her spaghetti and said, "I like it!" So that was nice. She also laughed at my punchline: "Neither, it's b-b-b-best to write w-with a pen!" which was even nicer.

At least Aisha was honest and just asked me the question. Kids are a bit better than grown-ups when they first meet me. They either ask straight out about my stammer, like Aisha, or just completely ignore it. That's the best, when someone doesn't even seem to notice and just waits till I'm done, knowing that I will get to the end eventually. Mum says a lot of the world's problems are caused by everyone being in such a rush and that I'm doing everyone a favour by forcing them to be a little bit more patient.

It's only when kids know what's going on with me that the problems can start. When they realize they can use it against me or laugh at me. Most of the time I just catch kids pulling funny faces at each other or giggling behind their hands as I am trying

4

to say something. But just asking a question about it like Aisha did, that's fine. I would rather that than deal with the frowny/smiley face that adults have when I first speak to them. An upturned mouth and a wrinkled forehead. I hate it when people look at me like that. I want to make people smile properly, not in the frowny way. I can see the moment when it clicks. When they get it, that what they are hearing is a speech impediment and not a choice. They almost look relieved, pleased with themselves. Then they get to show off how good they are at dealing with such a thing. In my experience there are four main categories of grown-ups:

1. The Encouragers

They have calm, smiley expressions and constantly say things like, "Go on", "Interesting" and, "I understand." Encouragers are OK. Although they can be annoying when they go too far and say things like, "Take a big breath in," and, "Relax." Telling someone to relax when they are clearly struggling is like shouting, "Run faster!" at someone being chased by a tiger. They would if they could.

2. The Mind Readers

This is the most common category and a very annoying one in my opinion. A lot of adults do this to kids anyway, even kids without a stutter, but they REALLY do it to me. This is the category who think they know exactly what I'm trying to say and so "helpfully" finish my sentence for me. They usually say something completely wrong. Most of the time I just go along with their version of the conversation, because I can't be bothered trying again. I ended up going to the toilet once, when I didn't even need a wee. The lady at the cinema ticket office obviously thought I was going to ask, "Can you tell me where the toilets are?" when I was actually trying to say, "Can you tell me where the popcorn is?" She took me right to the toilets, even though there was a huge sign and an arrow, so I thought I should go in. I didn't even end up buying any popcorn. I told Mum I had changed my mind when I slid back into my seat and she called me a "strange fish". That's the other thing that happens when you have a stammer. People think you're either thick or strange.

3. The Jokers

The most upsetting category. The grown-ups who don't know what to do and so choose to mimic me "as a joke". Believe me, this happens more than you would think. The other day I went to the shop and had to ask an old man in a brown cap to reach the chocolate milkshake for me. He responded by saying, "Y-y-y-y-y-yes, of course I can!" and then laughed at how funny he thought he was. I'm not sure why any grown-up would do this. It's almost too confusing to be upsetting. I still felt bad, though.

4. The Waiters

The best category and the one which you should try and be a part of, should you meet a stammerer. These are the rare people who don't mind waiting and will stay there for as long as it takes for me to spit out whatever piece of information I'm stuck on. Usually a new joke. You could be waiting a long time until I get to the end of a new one-liner. That's kind of how it works. The more I want to say something, the less my voice allows me to say it. It's like a sick joke in itself.

Obviously some Waiters are not so good. You wouldn't believe how obvious it is when someone's waiting but they don't really want to be. That's tough. I want to say to them, "Don't worry. Just go and do whatever it is that you would rather be doing. This is no fun for either of us." But I don't, as that would take even longer than whatever it is I'm stuck on.

As I turn back towards the mirror for another attempt – "My name is B-B-B-B..." – Mum pops her head round the door.

"Who are you talking to, Billy?" she asks.

"N-N-No one," I say, pointing to my reflection.

"Gosh, if only that mirror could talk. It must have heard all sorts from you!"

"Wh-wh-what's said to the m-m-mirror, stays in th-the m-mirror, all right?" I say in my best gangster voice. Mum's a pretty good Waiter. I suppose she has had plenty of practice.

"Well, you and your mirror can carry on chatting for ten minutes, then it's bed, OK? It's a big day tomorrow, you need your sleep." She winks at me and her head disappears from the doorway. If only I could be normal then starting Bannerdale High School would be easy. I'm going to try everything I can think of to get rid of this stammer, and become just like everyone else. Maybe even better than everyone else. Imagine that, I could be the most popular boy in school.

"You know that Billy Plimpton, he's the best and he's SO funny."

"Yes, everyone wants to be friends with Billy Plimpton. I think he's going to be famous."

"Tell us another joke, Billy, go on!"

Everyone will crowd around me at lunchtime, desperately wanting to be my friend, eagerly listening to my jokes ... if I can get rid of my stammer. I don't want to think what it will be like at Bannerdale if I can't.

I've made a list of everything I'm going to try to say like a normal eleven-year-old. I love writing lists. I write them for everything. I have a really cool notebook in the shape of a rocket, which is the perfect shape. I pin them up on the corkboard in my bedroom, ticking off things as I go, or adding new things when I think of them. It's jam-packed. I think I will need a new pinboard soon. Maybe I should ask for one for my birthday. Here are some of my favourite lists:

TOP TEN JOKES

This one is always changing. Number one at the moment is:

1. Why did the kid cross the playground? To get to the other slide.

THINGS THAT MAKE CHLOE CRY

This one sounds like a mean list but it's not meant to be. Chloe just cries at the most stupid things. So one day when I was bored I wrote a list. It makes me laugh so much reading it. Here are the current top three:

1. Blaming her for a fart she didn't do.
2. Telling her that unicorns aren't real.
3. Touching one of her teddies with my bare foot.

Here is my latest and most important list:

WAYS TO GET RID OF MY STAMMER

1. Practise in the mirror

My speech therapist's top tip. I like her a lot, but it hasn't worked yet. My stammer started when I was five. Mum thinks it was after I nearly drowned in a swimming pool. I'm not sure if I can actually remember being under the water or if I have just imagined a memory. Like when you remember something from a photo rather than from real life, or when you have just heard a story so many times you think you were there when you weren't. My feet feeling for the bottom of the pool and not finding it. Panic. Legs kicking around me and the muffled sounds of people above. I'm still not a huge fan of swimming.

Mum thinks I started stammering the next day. That's what she said to Sue. Apparently my great-grandad had a stammer too. Sue said sometimes it does seem to run in families. So that's what Mum always blames, a swimming pool and a great-grandad I never met. I'm not so sure about the drowning thing. I've seen video clips of me from way before that happened. Holding the rings for when Mum and Dad got married when I was three. Wearing a little waistcoat. There's one from when I was about four where I'm telling a knock-knock joke! Dad says I loved jokes even before I understood them. In the film I say, "Knock knock," and then you can hear Dad from behind the camera saying, "Who's there?" Then I say "P-Poo" and start laughing like a total weirdo. I don't even answer when Dad says, "Poo who?" I'm rolling around on the floor thinking that the joke is finished, even though it makes no sense. Dad says that just saying the word "poo" used to send me into hysterics. That must have been really annoying for everyone. I'm glad I have grown up a bit, and my jokes have definitely got better, even though I don't tell them to many people. I certainly wouldn't let Dad film me telling my jokes now, no way.

I think I can already hear the stammer on the video. It just got worse when I was five. Sue thinks that it may have "got stronger" when Chloe started speaking. (She always says the word "stronger" instead of "worse". I think it's so that I don't see my stammer as a negative, even though it totally is. Strong sounds nicer than worse.) When there was more chance of me being interrupted. That makes more sense than the drowning, if you ask me. I think

Mum doesn't want me to blame Chloe. It's easier to blame a swimming pool, or some great-grandad. It went away for a long time when I was six but then it came back again. That's when we started seeing Sue. I've been talking to myself in the mirror for about two years, so you would think if that was going to help it would have by now. Maybe it *is* helping and if I stopped having these lovely chats with myself I would get even worse! I'm not going to risk finding out.

2. Read a book called *Life Without Stammering* by Sophie Bell

Mum took me to buy some stationery and books I need for school and I secretly bought it with my book token while she was in the toilet. I don't want Mum knowing how much I need to get rid of my stammer, she will just worry and want to "talk it through" over and over. It was the only book on stammering that I could find in the whole shop. I tried to act relaxed when she came out of the loo, but my face went all tight and I bumped into a display on our way out. I knocked over a huge cardboard mouse and loads of books. Mum called me "a clumsy creature" and we had to stack all the books back up. I'm going to start reading it tomorrow.

3. Drink a herbal tea that I read about on the internet called *Matricaria recutita*.

(Try saying that with a stammer. I have – it didn't go well.) I read about it in a blog by a stammerer called John. He says it calms an "overstimulated brain". Maybe that's what I have. I'll drink it every day for a month. First I have to find a shop that actually sells it. I've been into both Tesco *and* ASDA and they don't. I have been saving my pocket money.

4. Pray to the Gods of Speech that my speech therapist, Sue, will find a magic cure.

This one is pretty unrealistic, as that's not what speech therapists do. They can't fix a stammer but they can help make it a bit easier. They give you things to practise and ways to breathe and they ask you about all of the things that you find tricky, not just with speech but with everything. Sue is really cheerful and kind, she has frizzy hair with grey bits near her head and she always wears necklaces that look like big colourful sweets. We haven't made much progress on the stammer so far, even though I have been going for years. Maybe as well as praying I should do my homework from Sue. Last time she gave me a booklet to read with loads of characters in it. They are meant to remind me how to talk in ways that can help my stammer. The Smoothies, they are called. There is a different one for each different technique:

- Slover is like a worm and is to remind you to go slow. Not a very imaginative name, I know!
- Big Softie (another genius name!) is to tell you to create soft sounds. A soft sound is when you try not to say a strong consonant sound at the start of a word. A bit like you are too bored or tired to say it properly. Try this – say "ball" without the "B" sound, but so it still sounds like you are saying ball. Weird, isn't it?
- Slick Slide blends into your words with a big "erm" at the start. So if you always get stuck on words that start with an S you could add an erm before it. Like ermsnake

instead of snake. Sue says that no one even notices if you do this but it feels really obvious to me. Why is "erm-snake" better than "s-s-s-snake"? I just want to be able to say "snake" like everyone else.

In the booklet there are pictures of them all. Big Softie's like a huge snowball with a blue scarf around him. Slick Slide is meant to be a "cool dude". Who says the word "dude"? Cringe. Sometimes I think adults who come up with these things just need a kid editor to check they are not saying something stupid, like "cool dude". I think the Smoothies are all a little bit babyish, to be honest, but Sue loves them. I wonder if she will still be talking about them when I'm twelve. I hope not. I don't want to be at secondary school and still be thinking about Slover and Big Softie.

Tomorrow I have to somehow make it through my first day at Bannerdale. If only there was a way to avoid speaking. Maybe I can communicate entirely through mime, like Charlie Chaplin. I'm sure that would go down well with a bunch of angry teenagers. Miming, "Please don't hurt me. I'm small and weak," as they stove my head in.

At least I'm starting from scratch in a whole new

place. I can be anyone I want, no one knows me. Maybe it will be totally different and I'll make loads of friends and no one will even find out that I have a stammer. But I'm also terrified, knowing that there will just be even more kids there to laugh at me than there were at primary school.

At least in primary everyone had kind of got used to me. My voice was normal to them so I could forget about it, most of the time. Mrs Jackson, my teacher, was OK too. She always picked on the same people to answer questions, which I liked (because I wasn't one of them) and she didn't care when I was drumming with pencils on my knees. (Unlike Mr Allsop the year before. He hated it! "Billy Plimpton, for the tenth time today: Stop that noise!") Year Six was the best because I was the oldest. (Not the biggest – I'm tiny – but the oldest, at least.) None of the kids from the year above were there any more, shoving me in the lunch queue, it was great. I got to sit on the Year Six benches in assembly, and we were allowed in the tyre park at lunch.

Ash was my best friend from primary – kind of. I'm not sure that I was *his* best friend, but he was definitely mine. He came to my house every Thursday after school because my mum's friends with his mum.

So he sort of had no choice but to be my friend, but I don't think he minded too much. He used to practise his penalties at me in the garden.

When we put Bannerdale down as my first choice on the application form I felt great, even though everyone else in my class is going to Hillside.

"Won't you miss Ash?" Mum said just before she clicked submit.

"I wiiill still see Ash. You seee his muuum all the time."

"I suppose so, honey. I just don't want you to feel alone, that's all."

I didn't tell her that I always feel alone anyway. That Ash didn't really hang out with me much at school. No one did. He tried to be part of the cool gang at lunch break. They all hung around the steps talking about YouTubers, while I shot basketballs with the Year Fives. That's the reason I chose Bannerdale, so that I could start again and get away from them all. I also didn't tell her that Ash says he won't be coming over after school on Thursdays any more.

On the last day of primary when everyone was signing each other's shirts he said, "Seeing as we are going to different schools now it's probably best if we try and make new friends, and anyway Mum says I can stay home on Thursday till she gets in. So I won't really see you any more. Good luck at Bannerdale!"

"Oh, OK," I said. "D-D-D-Do yooou waaant me to siign yoour..." But he had already gone off back to the cool gang. He was never mean to me, though, not properly, and he never once laughed at my voice.

The others sometimes did, when I was reading out in class or when I had to say "*baaa*" in the Christmas play. Mrs Jackson thought that it was the perfect part for me. She knew I loved jokes and so asked me to find some sheep jokes for the nativity. It was a good idea really, the sheep character always said, "*baaa*," to what everyone was saying and it always made sense, like Mary said, "Where is Joseph? Is he at the inn?" and I said, "*Baaa*," and pointed to the pub and it was meant to be a joke (like bar instead of baaa) but I could not even get the "B" out so it made no sense.

All the kids in the class were giggling, I think even some of the mums and dads were laughing and covering their mouths. It was one of the worst days of school and I couldn't stop thinking about it for the whole of Christmas. People's faces, laughing but not looking at me, mean mouths and rolling eyes, but not Ash. I looked over at him through my sheep mask and he just kept looking at me waiting for me to finish my

"*Baaa*." That's why he was my best friend. That's also one of the reasons I have to go somewhere new, where no one remembers the nativity, or all of the other times I got stuck. Maybe somewhere where I can find more people like Ash, who don't join in with the giggling.

That's my biggest fear about Bannerdale. Everyone laughing at me. I want them to laugh *with* me, at my jokes, not at me. But I can't even tell them any jokes until my stammer has gone. If I did they would be laughing for the wrong reason, just like in the Christmas play. I would be the punchline.

They can't laugh at my voice if they don't hear it, though, can they? That's why I'm going to try my hardest to keep quiet. Not say a word. Until I have made my way through the list. Until my stammer has gone and then I won't be Billy Plimpton, The Boy Who Stammers, I'll be Billy Plimpton, The Funniest Boy in School.

Wish me luck.

CHAPTER 2

Why do dragons sleep during the day?
So that they can fight knights.

I'm looking into the mirror again, yawning. My hair is like a nest and I have sleep in the corners of my eyes. I can see my Bannerdale uniform hanging up on the door behind me. It looks important, scary and exciting all at the same time.

"Good morning," I say to myself as I stretch my arms above my head. Then I lean in, thoughtful, looking harder at my reflection. My eyes aren't tight, my face looks relaxed. Different. All of a sudden I am wide awake. At first just a glimmer of hope, a faint idea that something could have changed. This has happened before, usually before a big event, when I know I am going to have to speak. I allow myself to get carried away and imagine a miracle has occurred. Maybe this time it's true. My heart starts to pound in my chest as the hope inside me grows. Has it happened? Have I been cured in the night?

"My name is Billy..."

I'm doing it. I'm really doing it! It's gone, my stammer's gone, and just in time for school! My stammer has GONE! Then I carry on: "...P-P-P-P-P-Plimpton." My heart sinks and I feel instantly and utterly ridiculous. I blow a big raspberry at my reflection.

Sometimes I wonder if it would be better to stop letting the hope sneak in. It just ends up making me feel sad. Fed up, I put on my new uniform and hear Mum shouting up the stairs for me to hurry.

After breakfast Mum keeps messing with my tie and saying things like,

"You look so tiny! You're too small to go to secondary school."

"Mum! Ssstop it!" I snap, buttoning my blazer up to protect my tie from any more twiddling.

Dad just smiles at me over his cornflakes.

Dad's at home now. All the time. He started a job at the local news place last week, filming the news and weather. My dad's a cameraman. He used to film sports events and so he was away *a lot*. He went to the Olympics last year. It sometimes felt like he wasn't really part of the family, not like the rest of us anyway, more like a fun visitor. Once, when I was meant to be asleep, Mum and Dad were arguing in the kitchen and I heard Mum say, "Jesus, Ian, it's easier when you're not here." She sounded really tired. I crept down and sat on the bottom step, to listen in, like I always do, until I heard Mum shut the fridge too hard and her angry footsteps came towards the door. I just made it up to the top of the stairs without her seeing.

I read a book once about a kid whose parents divorced and it started with secret night-time arguing. So when I heard them, that was the first thing I thought of. Sitting on the stairs, panicking, trying to think what I could do to stop it. Wondering if it was all my fault. Now I try my hardest not to think about divorce, but it always pops into my brain as I'm going to sleep. I haven't heard them arguing since, apart from about whose turn it is to empty the dishwasher, but I don't think people get divorced over cleaning the kitchen, do they?

Dad says filming news isn't as interesting as sports, "but sometimes there are more important things in life, Bill." I assume he means us. He seems really happy. Happy to be at home all the time, and Mum does too. They have started being really silly with each other. Mum hid in the laundry basket and jumped out at him the other day. Like they were kids. I'm pleased they're having fun, and glad that the divorce looks like it's on hold, but it's still a bit embarrassing.

The school bus stops at the end of our road. I had to tell Mum and Dad that they were definitely not allowed to wave me off on the bus. They wanted to bring Chloe and her pom-poms to the bus stop. Can you imagine? Could there be anything more embarrassing than your little sister, with her pink pom-poms, doing a dance at the bus stop with your mum and dad? They pretended to look really sad when I said, "No way!" and Dad started fake-crying really loudly. "But we love you!" he wailed.

The school bus is pretty cool. It's like a fancy coach with high-backed velvety seats. They don't use a proper double-decker bus as there aren't many kids who go to Bannerdale round here. I'm the only one at my bus stop in a Bannerdale uniform. That's fine by me.

From our class, just me and Skyla Norkins chose Bannerdale. She's a bit of a loner too. Everyone else is going to Hillside High. They wear red jumpers with the Hillside logo and they can wear whatever they want on the bottom. I saw a girl with ripped jeans, trainers and pink hair wearing a Hillside jumper, so the school really doesn't mind how you look! Not like Bannerdale. Apparently you get a warning if your shirt is untucked.

When I got fitted for my new uniform we had to go to the upstairs of this little sports shop through a brown door. I thought it was a very strange place to be buying school uniform. I asked Mum if she was buying me a fake. She laughed so hard I could see her fillings, but she didn't answer the question. It wasn't meant to be a joke. I sometimes get confused when Mum laughs – is she laughing with me, or at me? She didn't laugh at all when I told her my latest number one joke.

What does a meditating egg say?
Ohhhhm-let.

I mean, how is a meditating egg *not* funny? I pulled a stupid hippy face when I told it and sat in a meditating pose. I thought she would love it because she does yoga and is always trying to get me to meditate by putting stupid audiobooks on about floating through clouds with daft music in the background. They definitely don't relax me. They do the opposite. They wind me up.

She just ruffled my hair when I said the egg joke. I don't think she can have been listening properly. Maybe I need to work on my delivery. I'll try it again on Granny Bread – I test all my jokes on her.

Granny Bread looked so proud when she first saw me in my uniform. It's navy blue with a red trim on the collar and the Bannerdale crest on the front pocket. The crest is a peacock and it's beautiful. I keep touching it to check it's still there. It feels stiff and important. *I* feel important when I have the blazer on.

When Granny Bread first saw me in it, I thought she was going to cry. She kept touching my tie. "A proper uniform, with a proper tie. Not those scruffy Hillside jumpers. They look so uncared for. A proper school has a proper uniform, in my opinion."

As I'm waiting at the bus stop I see them all in their "scruffy" jumpers squashed on the other bus, on the way to their first day at Hillside. Hands pressing against the steamed-up windows. I see faces I know, like ghosts peering out from rubbed-out circles on the glass. The girls from the cool gang all looking down at their phones. A tiny nod from Ash as he notices me looking in. I feel a bit silly, like maybe

I should have stuck with him, with them all. They weren't *that* bad; maybe that's as good as it will ever be for me? Then my coach pulls into the bus stop and so I have to forget about them and start thinking about my new life.

There's loads of space on the coach so I sit in the middle on my own and sneak a look around. It's the usual, loud kids at the back, nerds at the front. In the middle with my bag on my knee is the perfect spot to remain unnoticed. Primary school wasn't totally useless. It taught me some very important rules for life. So important that they have made their way on to my pinboard so that I can remind myself whenever I need to.

HOW TO STAY HIDDEN

1. Don't go first

Too eager. Chloe always wants to do everything first and be at the front of the line, no matter what it's for. When we went to the dentist the other day and the lady said, "OK, who's going to go first?" Chloe jumped up and shouted, "ME!" like it's a good thing to have someone poke around in your mouth. I hate going first, no matter what it is. Let someone else get all the attention and then by the time it's my turn at whatever it is, no one will be interested in me. After the dentist had finished listening to Chloe going on about unicorns they didn't have much time to ask me any questions, so I got away with being silent.

2. Don't go last

Much like going first, going last is too much pressure. You always notice the kids who come in last from break and the kids who finish their tests last. Even the saying "Last but not least" says it all. What if you want to be "least"? I tell you what – go in the middle.

3. Don't sneeze loudly

My dad always sings, "Achoo, pussycat, whoa whoa," every single time he sneezes, which apparently is some old song. Mum laughs so hard every single time he does it as though she's never heard it before. I think it's the most embarrassing thing ever. Once he did it at school pickup, and everyone heard. The next day was a nightmare, everyone was pretending to sneeze all day! It was actually quite funny, but it did teach me never to sneeze too loudly.

4. Don't burp

Once in Year Four Hattie Hislop had something wrong with her and her burps stank like rotten eggs. Every time she burped she would start crying and that's when everyone knew to hold their noses. Honestly it was the worst smell in the whole world. She got better but no one ever forgot it. People were using it as a *would you rather* for years.

"Would you rather have burps like Hattie Hislop's or farts that electrocute you?"

"Would you rather have burps like Hattie Hislop's or worms as fingers?"

And for a while everyone's favourite, as they just could not decide:

"Would you rather have burps like Hattie Hislop's or speak like Billy Plimpton?"

5. Don't laugh - too much or not at all

Laughing too much = intense try-hard
Laughing not at all = deeply weird

Lily Cresswell used to laugh so much, all the time, usually at things that were not meant to be funny. When she read out a poem about the war in class (which was definitely not funny), she started giggling. I could tell that Mrs Jackson was getting really cross but that just made Lily worse. On the other hand Fraser Thompson never ever laughed and kids called him strange and dared each other to try and make him laugh. Anyway, thanks to Lily and Fraser, I know not to make those mistakes.

6. Definitely don't fart

No one will ever, *ever* let you forget it. I don't even need to explain this one. Surely every kid anywhere on the planet knows this rule? After the age of about seven farting in school is a terrible idea. I farted once in silent reading but luckily I was sitting next to Alma, who farts all the time, especially when we do stretches in PE, so everyone thought it was her. I felt a bit bad when they were all holding their noses and pretending they couldn't breathe, but not bad enough to admit it.

Lessons one to six could apply to any eleven-year-old in any school. Feel free to use and apply them when needed. Number seven is the biggest and most important rule. The rule that's just for me:

7. DO NOT SPEAK

Any of the things on this list can draw unnecessary attention. I don't want to alert anyone to the fact that I exist, but speaking is the big one.

I have brought *Life Without Stammering* by Sophie Bell in my bag. It could give me the answer. I could get off this bus and be a whole new person. I hold it in my hands and take a big breath in, closing my eyes. I make a wish. I check around and no one can see me; I've made myself really small. I don't want anyone to know what I'm reading, so I have ripped off the front cover, and am hiding the middle of the book inside the cover of an old *Dragon Quest* book.

I still feel nervous that someone might spot it from behind, look over my shoulder and read the words. I check behind and no one is looking so I relax and open the first page.

It's pretty boring. It doesn't tell me any tricks, or anything to do, it just talks about "self-confidence". How can I have self-confidence when I sound like a broken robot? I bet Sophie Bell hasn't even got a stammer. I flick through the pages and look ahead, through all of the chapters, and there are no lists, facts or rules anywhere. I shut the book hard and a kid looks over at me. Maybe I should add that to my Ways to Stay Hidden list.

8. Don't make any sudden noises or movements

I shove the book into my rucksack; it definitely won't work. Not in time for school, that's for sure. I wish I had bought the new Rick Riordan with my book token instead. That's number two crossed off the Ways to Get Rid of My Stammer list. Next I need to move on to number three – the tea. I just need to find a place that sells it. The thing is, I was hoping the book might give me something new to try for the register. I'm really worried about the register. I can be silent for a week, easy – apart from having to answer when my name is called. I have been practising different techniques in the mirror. I think it just made me more nervous, though. The pressure.

Have you ever noticed that when you desperately want something to go a certain way, it never really does? That is what I'm dreading, when I step off the coach and walk into Bannerdale for the first time.

CHAPTER 3

Why did the boy throw his watch out of the school window?
He wanted to see time fly.

I know that he's the one I need to watch from the moment I walk into my form room. You get a radar for these things after a while. He's sitting sideways on his chair, with his legs spread wide, as though he wants to take up as much space as possible. His tie is loose and I know he will get a warning for it, but he looks like the kind of boy who doesn't care about warnings. He *loves* warnings. He probably collects warnings and puts them on his wall at home like certificates.

He's whistling and looking around the room for his first victim. I avoid eye contact and sit as far away as possible. I see Skyla, sitting near the back, drawing, and give a little nod. She looks much less scruffy in the Bannerdale uniform than she did at primary. People used to laugh at her because her clothes were too small and her hair was really messy. Now her uniform looks massive but it's clean and her hair still looks a bit tangled but not as bad as it used to be. Maybe she brushed it for her first day.

Skyla is SO good at drawing. At primary she spent every single lunchtime sitting in the corner of the playground with her sketchbook and pencils. Once, when Jack Rouse snatched it off her and started throwing it around, it flew through the air and I got a glimpse of the most amazing faces looking out of the pages. Beautiful eyes but a bit scary too, like ghosts. She got her book back by punching Jack Rouse in the nose. Skyla doesn't care what people think of her.

I consider going to join her at her table but I can't sit next to a girl, that would draw too much attention.

Anyway, since the punch, I'm a bit scared of Skyla. So I choose a boy with floppy blond hair who looks pretty "normal". That's what I'm after, someone I can use as a human shield. Someone whose normalness might distract people away from me, make me seem "normal" too. The blond boy looks at me.

"Hi," he says casually and moves his bag so that I

can sit down. I just nod and smile, trying not to look weird by smiling too much. He carries on chatting to two boys sitting at the desk behind. They look like they already know each other pretty well.

I wonder if I've chosen the right seat when I look at the boys he is talking to. One of them is really tall. I mean, REALLY tall. I can tell even though he's sitting down. He looks like a cartoon character with his legs folded under the desk. His body is hunched over the top in a long curve. The other boy looks normal enough but he's rubbing his hands together fast like he can't stop doing it, and jiggling his knees under the table like there's too much energy in them and it has to come out. It's too late, I can't move now, so I sit and pretend to look through my bag.

I have a plan for the register. In the mirror, during the years that my reflection and I have been getting to know each other, my jokes and I have discovered that there are four different techniques I can use.

WAYS I CAN SPEAK WITHOUT
GETTING STUCK (AS MUCH)

1. Whispering

I don't know why but when I whisper I can say whatever I like. This only works when people are close enough, though. I whisper a lot at home. My latest idea is this: I want to try whispering into a microphone to see if my voice sounds loud enough. Maybe I could wear a secret microphone all day long. If it worked I could be a whispering comedian! "Ladies and gentlemen, please put your hands together and welcome to the stage ... WHISPERING BILLY!" Actually that sounds a bit odd. Maybe it's not one of my better ideas.

2. Singing

If only I lived in an opera, where they sing instead of speak, then I would be OK, but I can't exactly sing my way through life, can I? Imagine going into a shop and singing, "Please may I buy this Mars Bar?" People would think I was bonkers. Singing jokes is weird – I have tried it, it ruins them. Singing the register – even weirder.

3. Sleep talking

I didn't discover this one in the mirror, obviously. Mum told me. I used to sometimes sleep in bed with Mum when Dad was working away. She says I talk in my sleep and keep her awake. She recorded me once on her phone – it was hilarious. I was talking about putting something in a bin the wrong way round. It made no sense whatsoever. I didn't stammer in my sleep. That's the first thing I thought when I heard it.

I sleepwalk too sometimes. It freaks Mum and Dad out. Dad says he was up late watching telly once and I came in the living room and stood there like a zombie. Didn't answer when he said, "Bill, what you doing, mate?" He had to lead me back to bed and I couldn't remember any of it in the morning. Weird! Mum says it's because I have so much going on in my brain that it never relaxes. I don't get that. I reckon that I relax all the time, watching *Blue Planet* with Granny Bread or reading my favourite joke books.

She just thinks everyone should relax the way she does, lying in a bath with candles and a magazine.

If only I could be asleep when I answer the register.

4. Drumming

If I drum out a rhythm on my knees and say the words to fit the beat I usually stammer less. A few years ago I started doing it all the time. After a while it lost its power and stopped working so well. So I started drumming more and more. Harder and harder, to make it work again. Eventually Mum and Sue, my speech therapist, said that it was "probably a good idea to stop the tapping". Mum said, "You sound like a sat-nav, Billy, and you look like you have a problem with your movement." They thought that was worse than the stammer itself. One good thing that came from it, though: I realized I LOVE drumming. I practise my beats all the time, and I think I'm pretty good. I really want a proper drum kit but Mum says, "Absolutely no way!" She loves saying, "Absolutely no way!"

She says it to loads of things:

"Mum, can we get a dog?"

"Absolutely no way!"

"Mum, can I have ice cream for breakfast?"

"Absolutely no way!"

"Mum, can I get a drum kit for my birthday?"

"Absolutely no way!"

After assessing all the options, me and my reflection decided on a combination technique of raising my hand, whispering, "Yes, sir," and then clearing my throat, as though I have something stuck in it. The coughing explains the whispering and I should get away with it. It looked pretty believable in the mirror anyway. I'm not sure I can keep doing the same thing every day, but it will do for now.

"William Blakemore?" The teacher has started the register. The boy with the loose tie says, "Wassup."

Everyone laughs. The teacher looks at him as if deciding whether to tell him off and then goes back to the register. Now I know William Blakemore is definitely the one I have to watch. I need to be careful.

Next on the register is Matthew Coombes, the super tall boy who sits behind me. The jiggler is Josh Day and Alex Kirby is next to me. Alex has this plastic thing in his ear and I wonder if he's listening to music, even though it doesn't really look like an earphone. If I could speak I would ask him. When the teacher finally gets to my name I go bright red instantly. I put the plan in motion and I think it works pretty well, no one seems to notice. After the whisper and the cough, I sneak a look around me and no one is looking back. Perfect! I smile to myself. Maybe all of the practice in the mirror has been worth it. I breathe a sigh of relief and slip away to the morning's lessons. I won't utter a word for the rest of the day and will do the whispering cough technique at every register. Maybe secondary school is going to be fine after all!

For the rest of the morning, I spend most of my time wandering around the halls with my timetable in front of me. The most difficult thing about being a "Bannerdale boy" (as Granny Bread now insists on calling me) is not having a clue where I'm going. The rooms are all numbered weirdly. Art is in R1 and geography is in E11. I don't know what the R and the E stand for. If I were in charge I would get rid of the letters.

The Year Tens are supposed to be "looking out for us" and helping us if we are lost. They are too busy chatting in big groups or laughing at each other to notice me. That suits me fine, the last thing I need is some huge Year Ten asking me any questions and me trying to find an excuse not to answer them. So I just carry on wandering until I find where I'm supposed to be. When I get to Spanish fifteen minutes late the teacher just ushers me in and says something in Spanish. I sit down and bury my head into my bag. I can feel everyone staring at me.

I've got a new rucksack for all my books. It's really cool. Really big, so I can nearly fit my whole head in it. I don't, obviously, I think everyone would stare even more if I did that. It's black with little grey squares on it that look like pixels, and it has loads of pockets.

When I can't find my pen in my first history class and start panicking, frantically looking through all the compartments, the teacher, Mrs Able, is really kind. She has lines around her eyes that make it look like she's smiling, even when she isn't. She just knows without asking, smiles and quietly puts a pen on my desk.

I think it's a good name for a teacher. Mrs Able. I will start a new list: Good Names for Teachers. In primary school there was a reception teacher called Mr Friend. That's definitely top of the list. That probably means I need another list to go with it: Bad Names for Teachers. Dad once said that he had a teacher called Mr Fartlet and they all called him Mr Fart and then said the "let" part so quietly that you couldn't hear it, but loudly enough that he couldn't tell them off. I think you need to consider whether teaching is the right career for you with a name like that.

It turns out that I was right about William Blakemore. He messes about in every lesson, calling out and making comments. I can tell the teachers are all as wary of him as I am. I do my best to avoid sitting anywhere near him. If he's like this on the first day I can only think that he's going to get worse. When we sit back down for the register after lunch break Blakemore is messing with some of the girls' pencil cases and they are squealing at him to stop. Jiggly Josh walks past me to his seat and sees me looking over. "Blakemore is the worst," he whispers. "I went to primary with him, I should know." I just nod my head and pull a face like I feel sorry for him. I don't think he notices that I don't say anything.

The cough/whisper goes OK again for the afternoon register. We have a bit more time in form class after lunch, because the letters and timetables were handed out in the morning, and so our teacher Mr Osho tells us all about himself. He tells us he plays the trumpet and has a pug dog called Terence. He's brought his trumpet in for us to see. I really like the feel of it, cold and smooth, and the buttons feel good to press. It's much heavier than I thought. He loves jazz music and every lunchtime runs a club called Mr Osho's Music Lounge, where you can listen to music and play board games. I wonder if I should go.

I'm just thinking about how well my first day is going when I hear him say, "Now you all know a bit about me, I need to find out about you guys." Oh god, I have a horrible feeling that I know where this is going.

"So next Monday," he continues, "I want you all to bring in an item from home that tells me something about yourselves." I am frozen, staring at him. I can't believe what he is saying. "I'm giving you a few days to think about what you want to say. Tell us all a bit about what makes you ... you."

This clearly cannot happen. I won't need to say much before everyone in my new school knows exactly what makes me ME. I'm meant to be keeping quiet! Not "showing and telling"!

I should have a choice, shouldn't I? Like in primary when Ash didn't want to cut open a pig's eyeball, he didn't have to. This is like a pig's eyeball for me. I shouldn't have to talk if I don't want to. I start panicking and want to scream: "No! You can't make me. I won't do it!" Obviously I can't say anything, though. I just put my head down and ball my hands in fists, shaking.

I can't become a whole new person at Bannerdale. Not if I have to do this. Before I've had a chance to get rid of my stammer.

I need a new plan.

CHAPTER 4

Why did the teddy bear say no to apple crumble?
Because it was stuffed.

We are at Granny Bread's for tea, to celebrate my first day as a Bannerdale boy. She's making apple crumble, my favourite. We used to just call Granny Bread "Granny", but when we went out for lunch on Dad's birthday a few years ago Chloe got the giggles really badly when she heard Granny ordering granary bread with her soup. Chloe thought she was asking for "granny bread". So she has been called Granny Bread ever since.

I used to go to Granny Bread's every Tuesday after school and she always comes to our house on Sundays after my football match.

After our crumble we all squash on the flowery sofa, drinking extra-strong Ribena from plastic cups and watching an old episode of *Doctor Who*. Mum covers Chloe's eyes at all the scary bits. One of the kid actors in it looks a lot like Skyla from school.

"She looks like that scruffy girl in your class, Billy, what's her name?" Granny Bread says.

"Skyla."

"It's nice you've both got someone you know at your new school, isn't it?"

"Kind of," I say. "I didn't really talk to her today." I don't tell her that I didn't really talk to anyone.

I don't stammer as much with Granny Bread for some reason, especially when it's just me and her. Mum used to drop me off after school on Tuesdays and take Chloe to gymnastics. We played cards: patience and rummy. Now I'm at Bannerdale and Dad's back, I don't know if I'll still go round as much. I hope so.

Granny Bread looks at me really hard in the eyes and listens hard too. She is definitely a Waiter. Her eyes and ears are "going", she says, so she has to really concentrate on what I'm saying.

She's always lived on her own, or at least as long as I have been alive. My grandad died just before I was born. She says he was "a right old grump". So I don't think she misses him too much. I do think she must be lonely, though, in her hot flat all on her own. I wonder what she does all day. I think she really likes our Tuesdays.

After cards we usually listen to her favourite music on cassette tape while we eat our tea and then watch *Blue Planet*. Our favourite is episode two with the Dumbo octopus. It's called that because it has massive ears (like Dumbo the elephant) and it flies with them. (It doesn't actually fly, obviously, it swims, but it really looks like it's flying.) Granny Bread loves it! "What a strange creature, eh, Billy? Beautiful, though. The weirdest ones are the most wonderful, aren't they?"

It helps when someone looks at me like Granny Bread does. Stops what they're doing and looks right at me and listens. Not like when Mum is cooking the tea, listening to the radio, helping Chloe with her spellings and still pretending she's interested in what I'm saying. I still stammer, of course, even if you do look at me, but I like the feeling of being listened to.

Granny Bread LOVES my jokes. I tell her a new one every time I see her. She's the best audience member you could ask for. If I didn't have a stupid stammer I would be a stand-up comedian. I haven't told anyone that, apart from Granny Bread. If anyone ever asks me that stupid question, "What do you want to be when you grow up?" which grown-ups always seem to ask, I say, "An accountant." That seems to shut them up pretty quickly. I tried "bus driver" once but then they just asked me loads of questions about vehicles and I don't care one bit about vehicles so I asked Mum what the most boring job ever is. I don't even know what accountants really do – she said it's lots of maths. That doesn't sound too boring to me – maths is my best subject – but it seems to do the trick. I could never tell people the truth. Imagine the look on their face if I said, "I w-w-w-want to b-b-b-b-be a c-c-c-c-comedian."

I remember the moment that I realized it could never happen. Me and Granny Bread had just finished eating tea on one of our Tuesday nights and were getting snuggled on the sofa, about to watch *Blue Planet*. As we turned the telly on, a stand-up comedian popped on to the screen, telling a story about his dog drinking out of the toilet. I'd never seen a comedian on the telly before; I didn't even know that it was a proper job. He wasn't really telling jokes, like from my books, but talking about really funny

49

things that had happened to him. There was a huge audience, heads back laughing, wiping tears from their eyes, and him standing in front of the beautiful red velvet curtains of the stage. I couldn't believe it.

Sitting there with Granny Bread, I imagined myself standing in the centre of that stage, just like him, saying everything I want to say, without getting stuck. The audience cheering and laughing. There's no chance of that, though; it's a stupid thing to even think about. I felt cross with myself for even imagining it. Granny Bread could tell that I was getting upset.

"I want to see you doing that one day, Billy," she said. "Telling your jokes, making people laugh, I want to see it while I still can. I tell you, that would make me so happy."

I pinky promised her I would do it. Do a show just for her. She looked at me in the eyes and giggled as I held out my finger and showed her how to curl her wrinkly little finger around mine. I repeated, "Make it, make it, never never break it," over and over until she joined in and we carried on saying it, getting louder and louder until we both started laughing and couldn't stop.

"Oh, Billy, aren't we a daft pair?" she said, wiping

away a tear from underneath her glasses. I love Granny Bread so much, sometimes she seems like a little kid, how excited she gets about things. I *have* to keep my pinky promise to her, no matter what. I don't know how I will do a comedy show for her, but I will do it, even if it's just in her hot living room. After that night, I started watching comedians on YouTube. There are so many of them, and that's what they do as a real job, for money and everything. It's only made me want to do it more.

Tonight, I try and slip my latest joke into conversation without her noticing. That's the best, when you surprise someone. Especially Granny Bread.

"Granny Bread?" I say as casually as I can.

"Yes, sweetie?" she says, looking at me over her glasses.

"Last night I had a nightmare about being attacked by a shark..."

"Oh dear, do you think it's all the *Blue Planet* we've been watching?"

"No, it's OK, when I woke up I realized it was just a bream."

She laughs so hard, I wonder if she is going to choke on her crumble. Then I start feeling bad imagining myself killing Granny Bread with a joke.

It isn't until I get home that I remember the ME ME speech that I've somehow got to get myself out of. Time for a new list.

WAYS TO GET OUT OF THE ME ME SPEECH

1. Vomit or fake vomit on Monday morning.
2. Break a bone within twenty-four hours of the speech.
3. Set the alarms off at school just before form class starts.
4. Write a letter to my local paper saying that school is ruining my life. They will then start a pressure group called "Stop the Speech" and they will march outside the school on Monday morning holding placards and chanting until the school gives in.
5. Fake my own kidnapping.
6. Run away.

I'm aware that some of these ideas are more realistic than others, and that some may be considered excessive, but I'm fighting for my survival here. Maybe before I hit the list I'll start small: persuade Mum to tell Mr Osho that I don't have to do it. That sounds a bit more sensible. After the nativity from hell that ruined Christmas, Mum told my teacher that I didn't have to perform in the Easter show if I didn't want to. Of course I didn't want to, so I ended up playing all of the music from an iPad. That suited me fine. So it should be easy enough to convince her that the ME ME speech is not a good idea. I just need to make her see how bad it will be.

My plan is this. Over the next few days I'll become quieter and quieter and stop eating puddings. I LOVE puddings so Mum will definitely know there's a BIG problem. When Mum asks me what's wrong I'll say, "I don't know." This will carry on until she is *really* worried. Eventually she'll start guessing. When she mentions school I'll flinch, cover my eyes and put my head down and then she will know she's on to something.

Now here's the best bit, when she finally gets the truth out of me, it will be HER idea that I shouldn't do the ME ME speech, instead of mine! Then she'll write a note for me to take in on Monday. I'll go along with it, saying things like, "If you think it's for the best," in a sad, quiet voice and hold on to her hand while she cooks. I feel better already. Sometimes you just have to have a plan.

CHAPTER 5

Why don't farts finish secondary school?
Because they always end up being expelled!

I have been noticed. I knew it would happen eventually but I thought it would take longer than this. So far the only words I've uttered at school are, "Yes, sir," when Mr Osho is taking the register. So in a whole day that's four words. I've been there for two days and so I have spoken a total of eight words. I know what you're thinking... "This kid's maths is amazing!" I know, I know. Anyway, you would think that, with only eight words leaving my inadequate lips, I would have got away with it. NO. Apparently that isn't how school works.

This morning, day three, I'm sitting in the same spot as yesterday, next to Alex. As we wait for the bell

I am silently drumming with pencils on my knees. Facing the window, making sure that no one can see me. I'm doing it hard, so it kind of stings my thighs, but I like it. I'm practising my rudiments. They are like the basic rhythms of drumming.

I look up different drum beats on the internet and then practise with pencils. Until Mum changes her mind about getting me that drum kit, I have to practise with other things that are not so loud. I thought parents were meant to encourage musical tendencies. I could be a child prodigy, but I'll never find out. Not with pencils.

I look up when Mr Osho calls "Billy Plimpton" for what sounds like it must be the second or third time, judging by the tone of his voice. I'm so engrossed with the drumming that I've not heard the bell or even seen him come into the room. I completely forget my whispering/coughing tactic, panic and end up half-singing and half-stammering, "Y-Yes, siiiir." It sounds more like a noise than an answer. Everyone giggles and I feel my ears get really hot.

In maths I see William Blakemore watching me. Just like I have my radar for bullies, he has his for victims and it's gone off. When the bell rings for lunch and everyone gets up to go, he spins around and blocks my path to the door.

"Wass your name again?" he says loudly. *He knows. He's figured it out.* Time slows down. I'm in trouble. I can't run and I can't answer him. Some of the others are still packing up their things and a couple of them are watching us. They know Blakemore is trouble too and are probably glad he hasn't chosen to pick on them. I wait for as long as I can and then, when I know that I HAVE to do something. . . I shrug.

I know, I know! Shrugging does not seem like a good option when someone has asked you your own name but I have no choice! Just as he rises up even taller, clearly thrilled with his new find, I feel a hand on my shoulder accompanied by a loud, clear voice.

"His name is Billy Plimpton." It's Skyla! "Come on, Billy, let's go." She steers me out of the classroom and into the corridor before Blakemore can stop her. I'm about to turn and thank her when she skips off down the hall. I breathe a huge sigh of relief as I head towards the dining hall, but I know this is just the start. He knows my name now *and* I was rescued by a girl. This won't go down well with someone like Blakemore. Hopefully, if I can avoid him for the rest of the day he'll find another victim and forget all about me.

I sit in the far corner of the dinner hall on my own and eat my lunch as quickly as I can from behind my fake *Dragon Quest* stammer book. I don't read a word of it but keep peeking over the top to see if I can see Blakemore. He either has so much bullying to do that he doesn't have time to eat or I've somehow missed him.

After I have shoved in my chips I make a dash for it. Out in the hall it feels more dangerous than in the corner of the dinner hall and I instantly wish that I had stayed behind the safety of my book. There are kids everywhere, huge kids all in groups, playfully shoving each other around. I keep scanning the corridor in search of Blakemore but among the laughing groups and tall bodies I can't keep an eye on all of the doorways. I need to find a better lookout point, somewhere safer.

As I walk hurriedly past the theatre I realize I haven't seen it properly yet. When we did a tour of the school last year it was being rebuilt so we weren't allowed in. I peek through the little window in the door and I can see the stage. No one is in there so I look around and quietly sneak through the door.

It feels huge and smells different to the rest of the school. Grand. I feel so much better immediately. It feels like a safe place.

The red curtains are just like the ones that the comedian on the TV at Granny Bread's had, their huge velvet folds trimmed with gold. I push down a chair in the middle row, sit down and stare up at the stage, imagining all of the people who have performed there. Then I picture myself. Walking out into the middle of the stage confidently. Speaking clearly. Enjoying myself.

"My dad always says fight fire with fire," the imaginary me says as he struts about the stage, microphone in hand, audience hanging on my every word. "That's probably why he got thrown out of the fire brigade!" The audience love it, they roar with laughter, they love this version of me. I love this version of me. In my mind I carry on, "The other day I gave my best friend a massive rocket for his birthday and do you know what? He was over the moon."

I smile to myself, feeling my heart slow down and my shoulders relax. It's so quiet. I close my eyes and breathe in the smell. I can almost feel the warmth of the imaginary audience, hear their distant laughter.

Applause. Then the bell rings and jolts me out of my daydream.

As I walk towards the door, back into the real world, I see Blakemore's head pass by the window. I duck down, fast, praying that he doesn't see me. Heart racing again. Shoulders high. This isn't how I imagined myself at Bannerdale. Hiding, scared, alone.

At home I don't eat any pudding. It's ice cream. Mum gives me a funny look when I shake my head and push my bowl away. She knows I love raspberry ripple. Even though I know that my pudding plan is going to work I'm too busy thinking about Blakemore to concentrate.

In bed I look at the clock and it's midnight, but my mind is still whirring. When I eventually sleep I dream of Blakemore, pointing and laughing hard. Like he's never going to stop. I'm doing the show-and-tell speech. Mr Osho and the whole class are there too, all laughing so horribly at me. I wake up with a jolt.

CHAPTER 6

What lies at the bottom of the ocean and shakes a lot?
A nervous wreck.

We drop Chloe at school before we go to my speech appointment. It feels really strange seeing my old primary school. It looks so small! I feel like a totally different person now from when I went there.

Chloe is in Year Three and Mum still goes in and listens to her read in the mornings. I'm *so* glad I don't have to go through that torture any more. That was my worst nightmare. Reading out loud! We used to have this lady come in and listen to us every Friday. She wore lots of scarves all twisted around each other and dangly earrings that pulled down her earlobes. Whenever I got stuck she would say things like,

"Take a big breath in," and, "Slow down." Which, even though both of those things are supposed to help, only made it worse. It's a bit like when Mum is stressed about being late or getting the house tidy for guests and Dad says, "Calm down." She goes nuts. "Calm down! Instead of telling me to calm down you could help me, you patronizing twerp." Calm down is clearly not a good thing to say to someone who is stressed, even though that's exactly what they need to do! Human beings are weird.

When Mum gets back in the car she says, "Right, let's go, boyo," and then she whispers, "Shall we stop at the café after?" I smile and nod as she starts the engine.

We always stop at the Tastebuds Café for a toasted teacake after my speech appointments. Mum says it's a bit "naughty" but I think that makes the teacake taste even better. Sometimes if it's been a tricky session and I get stuck loads she even buys me a hot chocolate.

After my first ever speech therapy session my stammer disappeared for a week. Mum was so excited, I could tell. She thought it was a miracle. I kind of thought so too. Until it came back a week later. That's the really strange thing with stammers (or mine, at least) – it can totally disappear for a while and trick me into thinking everything's fine. That I'm cured. Then – *BAM* – it's back and it means business. It's like the cruelest joke ever.

The worst thing is that it's a little bit of *me* that's playing the joke. My own brain being so horrible to itself. I can't blame anyone else. Mum, Chloe or a swimming pool. I sometimes get really cross with it, with that bit of my brain. I tell it off: "Stop it! S-S-Stop it! I don't want you to do this to me a-a-any more!" Obviously I don't say this out loud. But I imagine telling it off and sending it away.

I told Sue once, "It's like I want to tell that bit of my brain to leave me alone." She seemed a bit giddy then. She clapped her hands together and started looking for some paper. "What a wonderful idea!" She made me draw a picture of that bit of my brain, turn it into a character and name it. I drew a little nasty old round creature with a stick. It was brown and green and had whiskers and a huge nose. I called it Bob. Then Sue drew a speech bubble and asked me what Bob would say. I wrote: *You can't get rid of me! I will never die.*

I didn't like looking at Bob after that. Sue made me imagine Bob packing a bag and me sending him away. I didn't want to, though. I didn't want to think about Bob any more. That took up a whole session. I kept thinking afterwards, what were we *meant* to do in that session? Before I gave her the idea to draw Bob.

I sometimes think Sue has no idea how to get rid of my stammer. She always asks at the end of the session, "So do you want to book in for another appointment?" I think sometimes she secretly hopes I'll say no. That I just remind her that what she is doing isn't working. That there is no cure. She's said as much. I just have to find ways to "manage" it. Well, I have found ways to manage it, tapping, whispering or singing, but they aren't always very useful.

Every time I go and see her I secretly hope that she has found an amazing new cure. A single magical tablet that I can take. That I'll walk out of her office and never stutter again. I always close my eyes and make that wish just before we walk in the room. Mum catches me at it today.

"What on earth are you doing?" she asks, as she sees me closing my eyes and whispering to myself.

"Making a w-w-wish," I say.

"Of course you are! Come on, we're late," and she bundles me in through the door.

When we see Sue today there's no tablet. She asks about school and I try to pretend it's all fine and repeat some of the things that Mum has been saying to her friends. "It's a l-l-long day but I have been getting the bus on t-t-t-time every morning and I really like my f-f-form teacher, Mr Osho." This looks like it's done the trick. Mum's smiling her big smile as though she has forgotten that she actually came up with these answers for me.

I've noticed this, that if you just repeat what an adult has said, they seem to love it. Sue asks about the other kids and I mention a few names, tell her that I sit next to Alex, and that Skyla from my old school is there. I don't lie but I definitely don't tell the truth either. I don't mention the speech. I don't want to ruin my chances of getting out of it and I know that she would want me to do it. She is always saying how I should "take every opportunity to speak" that I can, because, "You have so much to say, Billy, the world needs to hear what you have to say."

When she seems happy that school is going OK we have to throw a hedgehog ball to each other and say words as we throw it. We spend twenty minutes naming items of clothing and trying to say them as slowly as we can. I get the giggles when Mum says, "Bra." I start to feel a bit hysterical, as though I won't ever be able to stop laughing. I wonder if that has ever happened to anyone. I know that someone couldn't stop hiccupping for their whole life. That would be awful, wouldn't it? But what if you got stuck laughing for ever? It would probably make you sick and give you a tummy ache. Thinking about having a tummy ache does the trick and calms me down enough to carry on and say the word "jumper" as slowly as I can and then when Mum can't think of anything else we stop and Sue tells me how well I have done.

Mum always comes to my appointments. Dad has been twice but he's normally working. The first time he came I could see that he was getting too hot in the room and felt too big. He is six foot four and really doesn't like small spaces. I think he's pleased he doesn't have to come. Mum sits in the corner and smiles through every session. I always think her face must hurt after an hour of smiling.

There's one of those cool mirrors that people can watch you through, but you can't see them. It has a curtain over it and it was the first thing I ever asked Sue about. She always says that no one is watching us, "That's why the curtain's closed."

I stop listening to her today, when she's talking about Big Softie and the others. I imagine who could be on the other side of the mirror. Doctors with foreign accents, standing in long white coats, holding clipboards and wearing glasses. I picture what they are saying about me: "This is Billy Plimpton. One of the most tragic cases we have ever seen." Then I'm pulled back by the sound of Sue's voice. "Billy, are you with me?" I nod and look at the sheet she's holding up.

At the end of the session the room has got so hot that Mum's face has gone bright pink. We book another appointment in a month and then head for our teacake. Just as it arrives I remember my pudding plan and push it away, looking sad. Mum has an expression on her face like she knows I'm up to something. I just look away and cross my fingers under the table. Only four days until the dreaded show-and-tell speech.

CHAPTER 7

What did one plate say to the other plate?
Dinner is on me.

In the whole first week I manage to utter next to nothing. The teachers don't seem to be picking on people to speak yet. I think it's because they can't remember our names. When I hand my book in at the end of geography Mr Grant says, "Thanks, Bobby." I just smile and carry on. It must be hard to remember everyone when they have so many classes to teach, especially kids who are doing their best to be invisible. I obviously don't correct him. Maybe I will be Bobby for ever.

The cough/whisper technique is getting slicker, although I did notice Skyla looking up from her drawing at me today in morning register with a funny look on her face. She is the only one who knows the real me – the truth. I went red when I saw her and avoided her eyes.

At lunch, I see her walking over to my table with her tray of chips.

"Hi, Billy," she says.

I panic, do an awkward kind of half-wave and pretend that I've already finished, even though my plate is still full of pizza and I haven't even touched my cookie. I get up so quickly that I knock my chair over and the noise of it hitting the floor echoes around the hall. People are looking, so I just run out of the dinner hall without picking it up. My heart's racing and my ears are hot.

I don't want to talk to her in case other people hear me. I know that she helped me with Blakemore but I don't need her. I don't need anyone. I just need to stay quiet until I have got rid of this stammer, however long it takes. As I'm running away from her, I don't let myself think about the fact that maybe Skyla needs me. She sits on her own in every single lesson and I've not seen her chatting to any of the other girls in our class. She's nearly as silent as me. Skyla's tough, though. I mean, she punched Jack Rouse in the face! She's fine on her own, surely?

I just keep my head down, shut out any thoughts and keep walking. I feel my empty tummy rumble. I can talk to Skyla when I have made my way through my list and found a cure. I'm still on the hunt for the tea but no luck yet. We are going to Sainsbury's this weekend so fingers crossed they have it there.

For the rest of lunch and at afternoon break I just wander around. If you keep moving no one seems to notice that you are on your own and not speaking to anyone. I am wondering if maybe this will carry on for ever, maybe no one will ever ask me to speak. Do I want to stay like this for ever? It's a bit boring. Fingers crossed something from the list will start working soon and then I can start talking again. I bet Mum wouldn't believe me if I told her I had not spoken in a week. She calls me a non-stop chatterbox, but that's at home. Home's so different to school. Safe.

There are good things and bad things about being a silent student. I get to notice loads of stuff that other people wouldn't. Like at lunchtime I can watch people carefully choosing where to sit, who it's acceptable to be next to. Today, before Skyla sent me running, I saw Yasmin from our class deciding what food to eat, but when she went towards the vegetable bake another girl pulled a face like it's disgusting and so

Yasmin had pasta instead. Then I scanned across the tables, full of people chatting and trying to be the best versions of themselves. Swinging their hair over their shoulder or waving their arms around as they spoke. I saw a few kids like me, alone, just watching. I wouldn't have noticed all this if I was one of a group, waiting for my turn to speak. That's what everyone seems to be doing all the time, not listening to each other, just waiting until *they* can say something.

The downside of my silence is that it can get me into trouble. This afternoon I get lost on my way to English, and instead of doing what any normal kid would do and asking someone for directions, I just carry on wandering around. When I eventually find the room, the teacher's very cross.

"Come on. For goodness' sake, you should know your way round by now!" I try my best to apologize by widening my eyes and shrugging, but it just seems to make her more angry: "Sit down!" she barks.

I think maybe she's always in a bad mood, she has a sad mouth and squinty eyes for the whole lesson.

*

I've managed to get through the rest of the week without bumping into William Blakemore outside lessons. On Wednesday I have to run into a science lab at break time when I see him coming towards me in the corridor. A teacher in a white lab coat looks worried as I rush into the room.

"Are you OK, young man?" he asks, looking at me over his glasses.

I panic at the idea of answering him and try to look lost by getting my timetable out and pointing at it. I use it to cover my face as I head back out into the corridor. I feel like I'm in an old silent movie, in grainy black and white, with over-the-top expressions and exaggerated movements. As I turn the timetable the right way round and pretend to find the direction I need to go in, I almost jump and click my heels together, like they do in old films. The idea makes me smile. I don't do it, though, obviously. Imagine seeing a kid on his own doing a dance move. NO. NO. NO. That's definitely going on the list of things not to do.

The next day in English I know that Blakemore's watching me again, waiting for his moment to strike, so as soon as the bell goes I run. I sometimes hear him before I see him. Shouting things at people in the halls or singing loudly, like he wants everyone to know where he is. Then I run too, run away from the voice, and hide. I can't believe I've managed to avoid him for the whole week. It's not exactly what I want out of secondary school, to be constantly running away from someone, but it won't be for ever.

When the bell finally goes at the end of the day, I head out of the gates and on to the coach. As I slump into my usual seat in the middle I breathe a sigh of relief. The weekend at last. I am exhausted. It's hard work being alone, silent and avoiding someone. Especially someone you are terrified of.

When I get home Mum wants to go and celebrate the end of my first week at Bannerdale. We leave Dad and Chloe at home and she takes me to a new American-style diner on the high street called Uncle Sam's. We are sitting in a booth with green leather seats and a mini jukebox that holds the ketchup, when a girl with red lipstick and braces on her teeth comes to take our order.

"Hi, and welcome to Uncle Sam's. What can I get for you?" I go for cheesy chips – I just point at the menu and she writes it down.

Mum knows something's wrong with me by now. I have not eaten any puddings all week. On Thursday it was pineapple and custard, which I love, so she definitely knows there's a problem. When she asks if I want a milkshake I try to look as sad as possible and shake my head. It's not easy. I can see pictures of chocolate milkshakes with ice cream, wafers and toffee sauce. They look so tasty, but I just close the menu, push it away and keep focused on the plan. Mum frowns, but doesn't say anything. This is the moment the pudding plan is going to come together. I can feel it.

When she finishes her coffee, Mum pulls this funny face and takes a breath in and I know she is going to talk about something "serious". I think, *This is it, she's going to find out about the speech and let me get out of it.* For some reason my mind starts going through every other possible thing that she could say. What if it's got nothing to do with the pudding plan? If not, then why does she look so serious? Then she says, "Billy, Mr Osho called me today to let me know how you're getting on."

"W-W-What?" I say. "W-W-WHY?"

"He says that you have barely said a word all week."

"So?"

"He didn't even know about your stammer, Billy." She looks disappointed when she says this.

Before I started at Bannerdale, Mum had wanted to tell all of my teachers about it. I told her that I definitely did not want that, no way. I didn't want all my new teachers doing the frowny/smiley thing. I didn't want *more* attention on me. So I told her that I would tell them myself, I told her that she needed to "let me grow up", which totally worked.

"We talked about the show-and-tell presentation on Monday," she continues.

Oh no – she knows about the speech. This is not the way this is meant to be happening. My pudding plan is ruined and now she thinks I've been lying to her.

"W-W-W-Whaaaaaaat diiiid he saaaaay?" I asked. Even the idea of the ME ME speech makes my stammer worse.

"He said that you don't have to do it if you don't want to. He said you could just take something in to show but that you don't have to talk."

Did I say Mr Osho was nice? Well, he just went from being nice to being the best teacher that ever lived in the whole wide world. My head falls back and I pump both my fists in the air. Mission complete. Then Mum continues.

"But, Billy, I've spoken to your dad and to Sue." She looks into her empty cup and carries on. "We all think it might be a really good idea for you to try it. To face your fears. Sue said that if you want to talk it over you can give her a video call over the weekend. It can't be as bad as you imagine, it just can't. You can't go on not talking, sweetie. Anyway, won't all the kids notice if you are the only one who doesn't do it? I think you might be making things worse for yourself." She pauses and I know something bad's coming. "So I told Mr Osho that you would give it a go."

My throat starts feeling really sore and tight, like I have a fist in it. Tears begin forming in my eyes. I look at her, wondering if I can Go Nuclear. If Mum and Dad ever ask me to do something I don't want to do I have the ultimate top trump. I've figured it out. If I use the words "stress" and "not listening" in the same sentence I ALWAYS get my own way. It's like magic. It started after Sue once said that, "Stress and not feeling heard are the two main triggers for disfluency." Disfluency is another word for not speaking smoothly. She also said that in order to lessen stress levels I should "try and speak as much as possible in situations that may be challenging." That bit is not so helpful, though, when I'm trying to get out of something, so I just use the not listening bit.

I call it Going Nuclear. I don't use it very often as it feels a bit mean, to use my stammer against them.

Anyway, if I do it too much they'll catch on, but this time I think I need it. If they just stopped making me do things I don't want to then I would never need it, would I?

The last time I went nuclear was when we were all meant to go horse riding for Chloe's birthday. I can't even be in her room full of toy ponies; I definitely don't want to get on a real live horse. They kept telling me that I would enjoy it. I hate it when someone tells you to try something that you will clearly hate, like Marmite or avocado. I can't even keep track of the amount of times Mum has asked me to eat cucumber. I did start counting, I had a tally chart up on my pinboard, but got lost after about the fiftieth time. Just the look of their warty greenness freaks me out, I don't want to put any in my mouth! Even the word is horrible. *Cucumber.* It takes me a long time to get to the end of that word. Mum just goes on and on, "You might be missing out on something you love! At least try it once for me, Billy. Go on." Like she actually can't believe that anyone can think differently to her. I went nuclear on cucumber too, the last time she snuck some under my tomatoes. She looked a bit sorry when I shouted, "You never LISTEN to me! I feel so S-S-S-STRESSED out," and shoved my plate away. She's never done it again. I felt a bit bad, but she just would not stop offering me cucumber. What was I meant to do?!

I take a breath in and quietly whisper, "Mum, the idea of standing in front of the class makes me feel really STRESSED." I pause and take another deep breath. "I feel like you're NOT LISTENING to me." I feel really proud of myself for getting to the end and then I sniff and wipe my eyes for effect and look at her.

Something's wrong. I know straight away it hasn't worked. Has it lost its power? Have I used it too many times, like the tapping? She looks strong and stern and says, "I know it's stressful, and me and Dad will listen to everything you want to say about this. But I'm afraid we're going to stick to our guns. You know what Sue always says, avoiding speaking situations only makes it worse in the long run. You just need to do the speech in your own way. You'll be brilliant."

I feel like I'm going to faint. She has never sounded more sure of anything. Her face is set and for the first time in my life I know I'm not going to get my own way, no matter what I say. Then the tears start falling down my cheeks and I don't even try to stop them. I think about how scary the last week has been at Bannerdale. Always hiding and running away, constantly alone. I think about how scary it will be once everyone knows my secret, how much worse it will get, and the tears pour down my face. She tries to hold my hand but I pull away.

"You can't avoid these things, Billy. Not for ever. What kind of life would that be?"

"A b-b-b-b-b-better one than this one!" I scream. I don't care one bit that everyone can hear me. I'm not going to stay silent now. Not about this. I squeeze out of the booth and storm out of the diner, slamming the door on my way. I can see Mum trying to squeeze out from behind the table, getting her purse to pay and then follow me, but I'm too fast. I dash out and then run down the path between the shops.

When I know she's not following I stomp all the way to the park and sit by the lake, watching the fishermen. Tears still streaming. Rage and fear in every muscle. Thinking how much better everyone else's lives are than mine. Why can't I just be normal? Or at least just have a problem that everyone understands, like having to wear glasses, or verrucas on my feet. At least you can look good in glasses, sometimes people even wear fake ones. No one would pretend to have a stammer, would they? You would think that no one would ever *want* verrucas either, but in primary Ash once had one and had to wear a funny sock when we went swimming. I thought it was really cool wearing a sock in the pool and so I pretended to have a verruca too. When Mum looked closely at my foot she saw that it was just a dot of Sharpie on my toe and called me "a very odd creature". I am an odd creature. I bet no one on this whole planet would want to be like me.

It starts raining and I realize that I can't stay here thinking about verrucas all night. It's too far to walk all the way home and I don't know what number bus to catch. I look through my bag for my phone but I know it's not in there.

Most kids love having a phone but I hate it. Talking on the phone is the worst thing ever for me. It makes my stammer ten times worse, so even having a phone stresses me out. The idea of it ringing and me having to answer it is horrible. The person on the other end just hearing my grunting silence without being able to see what's happening. Even when other people's phones ring it makes my heart go faster. I always think they might say, "They want to speak to you," and then thrust the phone at me. Even people who don't know me. I have talked to Sue about this and she says it's really common to hate talking on the phone, which is why today when I actually need the stupid thing it's sitting in the drawer at home with no battery.

When I run out of ideas, I slowly head back to Uncle Sam's. On the way I walk past a shop called Beanies. In my rage I must have missed it on my way to the park. It's a health food shop – and in the window is a huge stack of different herbal teas! I can't believe my eyes. Sometimes when something happens that feels like it's a sign you have to just go along with it.

When I walk in, the man behind the till looks at me suspiciously, like he thinks I'm going to steal something. Especially when I am looking in my rucksack for my pocket money. I'm sure it's in here, I remember putting it in. My rummaging gets frantic and I start to lose hope, start wondering if I should prove the suspicious man right and just steal the tea. Then I find it in a tiny pocket. I feel relieved; I don't think I would be a very good thief.

When I eventually find the tea there are three types and I don't know which one to get, so I count my money and realize that I can only afford the cheapest. That's fine by me. I pay the man, shove the box in my bag and skip out of the shop.

I can't believe this is happening. Maybe it *is* a sign. Forget the stupid pudding plan, maybe that was wrong all along. Get back to the big plan. Drink the tea, get rid of the stammer NOW. In time for the speech. Show Blakemore that he was wrong, that there is nothing to bully me about, that he must have imagined it. Then I can get on with telling everyone my jokes and becoming a normal, popular kid.

Eventually I find where we parked. Mum's pacing up and down by the car on her phone. She looks like she has been crying and grabs me into a tight angry cuddle.

"Don't you dare do that to me again. I was so worried about you," she whispers and then strokes my hair roughly and kisses me on top of my head. I wait to see if she says anything else, but she doesn't. She definitely doesn't look like she's changed her mind about the speech. She gets into the car and I slide into the passenger seat. All of a sudden I'm aware of how puffy my face must be.

We don't look at each other and then as she turns on the engine, I say, "I h-h-h-hope they s-s-s-s-strap themselves in. Iiiit c-c-c-could bbe the longest sh-show-and-tell of th-th-their l-l-lives."

Mum laughs hard then. In a way I've not seen before. Not with me anyway. I've seen her laughing at Dad the same way. When he dressed up as a fish, for New Year's Eve, she laughed like that. But she has never laughed like that at me. When I tell my jokes, she laughs along with me, like she's doing me a favour, or like she's laughing for show.

This is different somehow. I should feel cross with her for laughing at me, but it feels good. Making her laugh. Like it will feel when I've drunk this tea and got rid of my stammer. This is what I want – to make people laugh. Just like this.

I start laughing too. It takes us ages to stop. She wipes her eyes, ruffles my hair and we head home. I can feel the shape of the tea box through my bag and it makes me feel happy. I can't wait to get home and drink some.

CHAPTER 8

Why is a stammerer like a teabag?
You only know how strong they are when they
are in hot water.

When we get back Dad repeats everything that Mum has already said to me about "running away". It's so annoying when they both feel like they have to tell me off about the same thing, like hearing it again will make any difference. If anything it makes me listen less because it's boring the second time round. Anyway, he wasn't even there! All I'm thinking about, as Dad's shouting at me, is the tea. The quicker I can get him to believe that I'm listening, the quicker I can have a cup. I look at him right in the eyes and pull a really sad, serious face. He clearly thinks I look sorry enough as he stops going on at me and starts looking at his phone.

I sneak into the kitchen and fill up the kettle. This could be it. The potion that cures me for ever. The kettle sounds louder than normal. I have never even noticed it boiling before, so why all of a sudden does it sound like it's taking off? I'm desperately trying to think about what I will say if they come in and catch me. They know I don't like tea, I tried it once and Mum got really cross when I spat it on to her favourite skirt. Luckily they don't come in, so I quietly take my Star Wars mug that Ash gave me for my tenth birthday out of the cupboard and put it by the kettle. I think my ears must be playing tricks on me when opening the tea box sounds excruciatingly loud as well. The rustling from the cellophane sounds like thunder. I cough and do it as quickly as I can and then shove a bag in the mug and pour on the water.

I cover the cup with my jumper, which I think is a genius idea, and head to my bedroom. As I'm closing my door I hear Mum downstairs saying, "What on earth is that smell?" I breathe in, my nose over the steaming cup. It does stink. But it will be totally worth it. I close my eyes and take a sip.

It's the most disgusting thing I have ever tasted. Worse than the tea I spat at Mum. Worse than the time Ash made me drink some water from the fish tank in primary school. (We were cleaning out the tank with a long tube and he double dared me to suck on it. What was I supposed to do – it was a DOUBLE dare!) That fish water was delicious compared to this stuff. It's even worse than the time Granny Bread made hot chocolate with salt instead of sugar. I tell myself it will be worth it and pinch my nose and take another big gulp. I can feel all the bumps on my tongue pop up as the heat from the water scalds my mouth. I should have added some cold like Mum does into her peppermint tea at bedtime.

After blowing and waiting, I eventually finish the whole revolting cup, and I look into the mirror to see if it has worked.

"Th-th-th-this b-b-b-better be w-w-w-w-worth a b-b-big throbbing red b-b-b-burned t-t-t-tongue," I say to myself, stammering even more than normal.

I feel disappointed and really, *really* silly. As if one stupid cup of rank tea was going to change everything. I don't know what's wrong with me. Sometimes when you want something so much, you can make yourself believe it's possible, even when it's not. Like when England are in the football World Cup and the whole country goes nuts, putting up flags and singing songs, and then we get knocked out in the first round. It's that stupid feeling again – hope. I hate hope.

I'll keep drinking it, though, in as hopeless a way as I can. There are still three days until the speech. Maybe it takes a few cups to work.

The next day I make another cup, sit down, and try and write something to say for the ME ME speech. I freeze. I don't have a problem with writing. Actually, I like it. The feeling of writing. The feeling of someone reading my words and hearing what I have to say. Properly hearing, with nothing getting in the way. But writing something that I know I have to stammer out loud feels *very* different. Terrifyingly different. I push the paper away and sip on the tea. It really does taste like sludge.

I manage to drink eight cups, until I can't cope with any more. I barely leave my room all day apart from sneaking into the kitchen to boil the kettle. After cup number three, I stop testing to see if it's worked in the mirror and just stay quiet. It's clearly not working, and I can't cope with looking at myself and hearing my stupid voice any more.

That night I sit down with a blank piece of paper to plan what I might say. I get hot and my hands start shaking. It is not a good sign. The speech is going to be bad, I just know it. I look up at the pinboard and there is the list staring back at me: Ways to Get Rid of My Stammer. I look at all of the options, angrily crossing them off as I go through them one by one.

1. Practising in the mirror is just making me hate myself even more.
2. The stupid book is pointless, it has loads of words I don't understand in it and basically the bits I do understand say, "Get used to having a stammer." That's not a cure!
3. The tea's useless and minging.
4. There is no point in praying that Sue finds a cure. I'm not seeing her for another three weeks.

Then, as I'm scribbling out the words, I remember what Mum said in the diner: "You can give Sue a video call over the weekend." I look up to the sky.

"Please, Gods of Speech, whoever you are, let Sue have found the answer."

I run downstairs and get my iPad from the drawer and head straight back up to my room. Sue's been wanting to Skype me for ages. She thinks that doing video calls is a good way to start dealing with my fear of talking on the phone. She gave me her Skype name and said, "If you ever have a question or want to discuss something between sessions then I will do my best to answer."

I click the button to call and then see my face pop up in the corner. It's a bit like talking to myself in the mirror, I think, and then Sue's face pops up large underneath mine. "Billy, how lovely to hear from you!"

All of a sudden I feel a bit stupid. I haven't even thought about what I'm going to say to her. I can't exactly say, "Hi, Sue, just wondering if you've found a cure over the last week?", can I? So I settle for a simple "Hi" and let her do the talking. I'm sure she will tell me if they have created a new magic medicine in the last few days.

"I spoke to your mum yesterday and she told me about school and the show-and-tell on Monday." I nod. I feel a little bit like I might cry but I just squeeze my hands tight in a ball.

"Have you decided what you might want to show to everyone?"

I shake my head.

"Just think about something you love, Billy. Something you would love for people to know about you. When you have thought of something that you feel passionately about, the words won't feel as important. Does that make sense?" I nod, wishing I had never called her. There is no cure and no way out of this.

"Even if you just practise a few words in the mirror, a sentence or two, using all the techniques we use in our sessions, you will feel more prepared. You never know, you may end up wanting to say more!" I don't think Sue really gets how bad my stammer is in real life. Outside the small office with the two-way mirror. I asked her once if she had ever had a stammer and she said, "Everyone stammers sometimes, but, no, I have never had a stammer that has impacted my life." I need to get her off the screen and so I force myself to say, "Th-thanks, Sue. I will s-s-see you s-s-s-s-soon," and click the little button so that we both disappear.

I can't do this. The stammer is not going away by Monday, that's for sure. I tear the list from the pinboard and rip it into pieces. As I look back up at the board I see the words: *Ways to Get Out of the ME ME speech*. As I am running through the options, there is just one possibility left. I grab my rucksack and start packing.

Maybe it's time to resort to number seven.

7. Run away

I have packed enough socks and pants for a week and some chocolate that I've had hidden in my wardrobe since Easter. I shove my sleeping bag in and throw it on to my back. Standing at the top of the stairs wondering how to sneak out, I hear Mum and Dad laughing in the kitchen. They sound so happy. As I creep down the stairs I start to feel really sad and scared. I tiptoe to the side door and silently take the spare key from the top of the picture of a cow, and it turns effortlessly in the lock as if it's making my escape too easy to turn back on. Part of me wants them to catch me leaving, to hug me and tell me that I don't have to do the speech, that I don't even have to go back to Bannerdale ever again, but I know that won't happen and so I step out into the rain.

When I stand on the pavement I realize that I have no idea which way to go, and so I just stand there getting wetter and wetter. Eventually I sit down on the curb and let the water trickle down my neck, drenching my T-shirt. *I can't even run away properly*, I think, as I look back at the house, wondering when they will even notice that I'm gone. *What's wrong with me? Why can't I do anything right?*

I must sit there for about an hour, as by the time I admit that I'm not going any further I'm shivering with cold and every inch of my body is soaked. *I would feel even lonelier on a park bench.* Imagining myself in my sleeping bag on a bench in the rain is too much. It's hopeless. There is no way out of it; I stand up and head back towards the house.

When I quietly let myself in I can hear Mum and Dad still talking in the kitchen. No one even noticed I was gone, that's how invisible I am. I stomp up to my room and sit on the bed, my bag still on my back. I can hear the rain pouring outside. I *have* to do the ME ME speech. All I have to do is stand up in front of the class. They are going to find out about me sooner or later anyway, if not in the show-and-tell then some other way. I was stupid to think that I could keep it hidden. I don't know what I'm going to do, but suddenly I feel exhausted and all I want to do is sleep. So I lie down in my wet clothes and dream of nothing at all.

As soon as I wake up, I'm thinking about the speech. I decide to give the tea one final chance and sneak another cup upstairs. As I'm sipping the revolting stuff and looking at my blank paper, the pen sitting on top waiting to write, I'm thinking about what Sue said. What do I love?

Then it happens, like a bolt from the sky.

An idea.

I laugh out loud. This can't be it, can it? Is this the thing that will save me, that will make it all OK? Maybe, just maybe, if I can do this then everything will change. I won't have to be silent any more. I won't have to run, from Blakemore, from Skyla, from the restaurant, from my home. I'm always running away; maybe I can stop running and start facing everyone, like I'm facing myself now in the mirror.

"You can do this, B-Billy," I tell myself and for the first time in a long time I believe in what my reflection is saying. Maybe it *was* the tea, maybe my prayers and my chat with Sue did it. I grab my joke book off my shelf and my favourite green Sharpie and run downstairs to get some cardboard. It's exciting to have a project. If I don't finish it before football I will do the rest tonight. I've got until the morning, even if I have to stay up all night to get it done!

CHAPTER 9

What is a goalkeeper's favourite snack?
Beans on post.

I know, I don't seem like the kind of kid to play football. I'm not. Dad was the one who made me join the team in the first place. Every week he says the same thing: "It's good to be part of a team." I'm not so sure. It's only good to be part of a team if the team wants you to be a part of it, surely? My team, the Hartwell Heroes, don't really have a choice. They needed extra players so Dad signed me up last season without even asking me! We ALWAYS lose. I'm not even joking. We have NEVER won a match. Last season we were so desperate to score we started practising a team goal celebration. After each game we would spend ten minutes adding new bits to our moves. It started with Martha doing a backflip and then everyone added their own stuff. It took us eight matches before we scored and by that time it was nearly a proper dance routine. Luckily I got out of it because I'm in goal. You would not catch me dancing around a football pitch when the final score was 10-1 to the other team.

We watched the World Cup on the telly together last year. That's what gave Dad the idea to sign me up for the Hartwell Heroes. He wasn't away filming the World Cup for a change and was really excited about watching it together. It was fun, we shouted and ate crisps and he drank beer. We had a big chart that we wrote all the scores on.

I like watching football but am not so keen on playing it. I don't like tackling people and I *really* don't like being tackled. I avoid the ball. Not a great tactic for success, but good if you want to keep your shins in one piece. I don't think I'm being weird here.

These are some things kids are always told:

Do not hurt anyone.

Do not get too physical.

Do not take things without asking.

Always share.

Do not shout at each other.

Then all of a sudden it's OK to shout and shoulder barge each other out of the way in order to "keep possession". It's fine to "attack the ball" and "get in there".

Parents turn into hooligans when they watch football. Once I heard Jay Riley's dad tell him at half-time that he was being "too polite". (Jay had apologized for bumping into someone who had the ball. But that's just good manners!) Then I heard him say, "Take the ball. Don't give them a chance! It's not their game, it's yours." (It definitely was their game. We were losing 8–0.) Jay did not look convinced, like his dad might be tricking him, so his dad went further: "Jay, it's OK to get involved. You don't need to say sorry. In fact, even if you foul someone it's OK." He was getting excited with his speech now. He had Jay by the shoulders and was holding him a bit too hard. "It's *more* than OK." I could see he was building up to something, he looked around and whispered, "You know what, buddy, if you foul someone I'll give you a fiver." Jay looked around to see if anyone was listening and whispered, "Are you serious, Dad?" I put my head down and pretended to sort my shin pads out. "Yeah," his dad went on. "I'll give you a fiver if you foul someone. Go on, son, get in there. Make it count."

When I told Mum all this she said that it was "terrible parenting" but she laughed at the same time so I'm not sure if she meant it. Jay got a yellow card in the second half for a sliding tackle. I don't know if he ever got his fiver. I hope he did.

When our coach realized that I would always be "too polite" for the game he put me in goal. You would think that it's the worst place to be when we lose every single week, especially at my height! I'm the third shortest in my class. But weirdly I quite like it in goal. When I see someone heading my way it's like time slows down and all that matters is the ball. Obviously I let a lot in, but I stop a lot too and my goal kick's really coming on. I can nearly get it to the halfway line now. The others think I'm OK too. Either that or they just really don't want to be in goal so they are being kind to make sure I don't leave.

Mum can't watch the matches any more, she says it's "too stressful". Dad loves it, though; when he comes he shouts all the way through: "That's it, Billy. Hold your position! Put some pressure on!" I don't know why he shouts so much, it's not like anyone's going to listen to what he's saying. You can't learn new skills when you are in the middle of a match.

It's like trying to tell someone how to cook a lasagne when it's already in the oven. It's too late.

Chloe's here today with her stupid pom-poms. I tried to ban her, it's too distracting, but she cried and Mum said I was being cruel. I can hear the rustling and see the pink strands bouncing about out of the corner of my eye. It's too busy. It feels like she's going to cheer all of my mistakes. *I* wouldn't be allowed to go and put *her* off in gymnastics, so I don't know why it's OK for her and her pom-poms to put me off. Sometimes things really are not fair, but Mum and Dad don't seem to get it.

As I'm on the bench getting my shin pads on I hear a voice above me.

"Hiya, Billy." It's Alex from my class, wearing a blue Beeston Rovers top. I feel really strange seeing him here, like school and football are two totally separate worlds. I don't know what to do so I just nod and smile. "I didn't know you played," he says.

I'm not sure whether to answer him or not. Can I speak outside school? I occasionally talk to the kids on my team, but they've known me for ages, what about my vow of silence? Luckily he just carries on, "I'm only ever a sub, they never let me play more than five minutes. I can't blame them, last time I played I scored two own goals! One would have been OK, but two?! That's how bad I am."

I laugh then without thinking, and hearing the sound of my laugh is awkward. It's OK to laugh, though, isn't it? You can't stutter when you laugh. Maybe I need to add that to my ways of not stammering. Singing, whispering, laughing. I make a mental note to try and laugh some words out into the mirror when I get home to see if it makes a difference.

"Anyway, good luck! I hope you're better than me! Watch out for Blakemore, he's pretty rough. I'm glad I don't play much; I think he would probably foul me if he got the chance, even though we're on the same team!" He's laughing at this, but I've stopped listening after the word *Blakemore* left his lips, I'm too busy scanning the field, panic rising in my chest.

Sitting on the grass in a Number 7 Beeston top, getting his boots on, is William Blakemore. I had no idea he played football! Standing over Blakemore, eyes fixed to his phone, is an older kid, who looks just like him. The same oversized frame and big features. He looks even meaner than Blakemore, his face set in an angry frown. I decide it must be his brother, and thank my lucky stars that he's not playing too. As Blakemore gets up I see the older and meaner version grab at the back of Blakemore's shirt and pull him back, force him into a tight, painful-looking hug and say loudly,

"Good luck, bro. Break a leg!" And with that he shoves him on his way, kicking out at the back of his legs so that he stumbles.

I see Alex looking over at me. I nod to him, duck behind a picnic bench and wait there, pretending to do my boots up, until it's time to start the match. When Blakemore's far enough away I sneak into goal without him seeing.

Luckily he's in goal too, so we're as far apart as we can be. It isn't until halftime when we're losing 10–0, that he sees me.

"Billy Plimpton! I wondered why their goalie was so bad. It's you!" Then he hugs me so tight that I can't breathe properly and slaps me on the back really hard. Anyone looking must think that he is genuinely pleased to see me. When Coach calls me over he lets me go, adding another hard slap on my back as I go.

When I'm back in the goal and the whistle's being blown for the start of the second half I can still feel the shape of his hand on my skin. He is playing up front now and so is much closer to me.

I can hear Chloe shouting, "BILLY! BILLY! BILLY!" at the top of her voice as she shakes her pom-poms about and I desperately want her to stop. Blakemore gets the ball and copies her, "BILLY! BILLY!" as he's heading towards me. I don't know whether I should try and save it or not. I don't want to make him angry with me. Luckily I don't have much choice as he kicks it high over the net. He comes towards me and for once I can't run.

"How long have you been playing, BILLY PLIMPTON?" I hate the way he says my name. I just look at the ground. "Answer me, then," he spits. I don't say anything, my cheeks are burning. "Are you an idiot? Why can't you speak?" he says. Then the ball comes back to me for the goal kick.

As I place it down the referee shouts for Blakemore to give me some space. He walks past and shoves me hard, pretending that he's bumped into me by accident. His hands high in surrender, a fake look of apology on his face. As I land on the ground the referee blows his whistle and shows Blakemore a yellow card. I look up and Alex is smiling at me sadly from the bench. At least he isn't laughing.

"Did BILLY PLIMPTON just get me a yellow card?!" shouts Blakemore at the top of his voice. "Don't worry, Billy. I'll see you at school tomorrow. See what you've got to say about it then."

CHAPTER 10

What object is king of the classroom?
The ruler.

As I'm heading out of the door Mum hugs me tight. "I am so proud of you for doing this, Billy. I know it's not easy but we are OK, aren't we?" I nod. "You haven't even told me what you're going to talk about!"

I smile and say, "I wiiill t-tell you later," and grab my bag.

"My amazing boy." She always says things like that: Amazing. Incredible. Remarkable. Wonderful. Astonishing. According to her I'm all of these things. I don't really want to be any of them, though. I just want to be normal.

William Blakemore hasn't brought anything in and so "shows" his pencil case and says how "important" it is to him. Then he throws it up into the air and it lands on the floor. Some kids laugh as he takes a massive bow as he picks it up.

"Well, thank you, William," Mr Osho says. "They always say you can tell a lot about someone by their … pencil case. It must have taken you a long time to come up with that."

"Hours, sir." Blakemore grins. I'm shaking. I try not to think about what Blakemore will do to me after this.

"Next up," says Mr Osho, looking at his register, "is Alex."

Alex shows us his hearing aids. He tells us that he lost his hearing when he was four and that he mostly uses lip reading but his hearing aids mean he can hear a little bit in his left ear.

"But," he says, "if you're not looking at me then I probably won't hear you. Either that or I'm just ignoring you!"

Everyone laughs when he says that. He high-fives Josh and Matthew as he sits down, and smiles at me. He seems proud. It's kind of amazing. I wish I could be more like that. I try and breathe in some of his confidence.

Everyone else has brought in computer games,

teddies from when they were little or photos of their pets. When it's Skyla's turn she shows us a tiny silver bracelet that was her baby sister's, who died when she was an hour old. Even though I've been at school with Skyla for so long I didn't know about it. I think it's a really brave thing to talk about. Mr Osho looks like he's going to cry, but Skyla seems OK. She says it happened a long time ago. It makes me feel bad for being so nervous. If she can talk about that then surely I can do this.

Yasmin Ohri is up before me. She's brought in a photo of her family and is talking about how important her friends are, how they are like her family too. Then she makes a heart shape with her hands at the end. The girls all whoop and clap. I'm sitting with my cardboard between my knees, still trembling with fear.

I wish my name wasn't Plimpton. It means I'm always near the end of the register, so I have longer to worry.

Mr Osho waits for Yasmin to sit down and then says, "Next up is Billy?" He gives me a little wink and starts a round of applause. I stand up and slowly go to the front. I avoid looking at William Blakemore. No plan, however good, will stop him from making me nervous.

Instead I focus on Mr Osho and Skyla because they are smiling at me. I take out my favourite joke book, *999 Jokes for Kids,* and hold it up for the class to see. Then I raise my first sign. In big chunky letters it reads:

**MY NAME IS BILLY PLIMPTON
AND I HAVE A STAMMER.**

I see my hand shaking like it doesn't belong to me. I put down the card, and pick up number two, and then number three:

I BROUGHT IN A JOKE BOOK...

...I LOVE JOKES.

The room is so quiet. Five more signs to go.

**UNFORTUNATELY I CAN'T
TELL YOU ONE TODAY.**

**IT'S HARD TO TELL A JOKE
WHEN YOU CAN'T GET TO
THE END OF A SENTENCE.**

I hear a couple of the girls say, "Ahhh," and, "Bless him."

THE END.

I bow and then hold up the last two signs.

NOW YOU CLAP AND CHEER...

They are doing it! They're actually clapping and someone whistles. I look at Mr Osho; I'm worried that he'll think I have cheated, that my signs are only showing and not telling, that he'll ring my mum and tell her that I didn't speak, but he has a big smile on his face and I know it's OK. I hold up my final sign.

...AND I BECOME THE COOLEST KID IN THE SCHOOL.

Everyone laughs hard at the last sign and I take another bow and go back to my seat. Alex holds his hand up for a high-five and then Josh and Matthew do the same. My head's fizzing and my ears are getting hot. It feels good though. People really laughed! I'm almost relieved. I don't have to hide my stammer any more.

When I look up I see William Blakemore staring right at me. I try to pretend that he isn't, to lie to myself and enjoy the moment. For now all that matters is that I've done it! I've done the speech and it was OK! Better than OK, they laughed! Maybe next time I'll try and say the words out loud.

On my way out of class Mr Osho calls me back and waits for the classroom to empty.

"How are you feeling, Billy?" he asks, smiling.

"OK, I think."

"That was an incredibly brave thing to do, buddy ... and properly funny too. I'm so impressed with you."

"Th-thanks."

"Now, I need to admit something. In all my years teaching I have never taught anyone with a stammer before, can you believe that?"

I just smile and shrug and he carries on.

"So I need your help, if that's OK? Can you let me know any things that would make it easier for you? Things that people do that are annoying or make it more difficult. I want to know them all."

I just nod, thoughts rushing into my head about

Waiters and Encouragers, but I know that I'm not about to start explaining all that to him now.

He looks at me and almost like he can read my mind he says, "I know there must be loads of stuff and you're not about to launch into a monologue about your entire life experience! So how about this..." He rummages around in his desk and brings out two little notebooks, one has blue stripes and the other has drum kits and the words *BOOM* and *CRASH* on it.

"Pick one," he says.

I immediately point to the drums.

"I thought you might go for that one. I've seen you drumming away with your pencils! I used to drum, you know, before the trumpet. I wasn't very good and it was years ago but I could show you a few bits and bobs on the school kit sometime?"

"Yes, please!"

"Great. Now, in this book, if you think of *anything* at all that would be helpful for me to know, just jot it down, OK? It's not a workbook so it can be as messy as you like, and you can doodle in it or whatever you want, but if something pops up then write it down and I will check in with you at the end of each week. Sound good?"

"Yeah. Th-thanks, sir."

As I'm about to walk out, clutching my new notebook, I think of something and stop and turn around. "A-A-Actually, sir, th-there is one th-thing that I can th-think of now."

"Go on."

"Iiit's qu-qu-qu-qu..." Mr Osho just waits as I'm stuck, "quite hard being at th-the end of the r-register."

He pauses and thinks for a moment. "Because you have to wait so long?"

"Yeah, I would r-rather g-g-get it over and done with," I say, quickly adding, "B-B-B-But not first either!"

"Yes, I can see that. No worries, that's an easy one to fix. I will send a message round to all your teachers and we will move you up the register. In fact, maybe I will get the whole register changed so that it goes on first names, then you'll be near the start and everyone else will be shuffled round too so that it's not just you who's moved. Sound good?"

"Really?" I say.

"Of course, Billy, that's an easy change to make. That's why I want you to tell me everything. You can't have a good time at school and learn loads if you're stressed out, can you? I want happy kids in my class!"

"Th-thanks, sir," I say, looking down at my

notebook and feeling like this day just keeps getting better and better.

At lunch Skyla comes and sits with me and I don't feel like I need to run away.

"I loved your speech," she says, shovelling some chips into her mouth. She looks really hungry.

"I liked yours too," I whisper. "I'm sorry about your sister, I never knew.'"

"Thanks. Mum's been pretty messed up ever since, she spends most of her time in bed, but I'm OK, I can look after myself."

I don't know what to say then but it feels good to have said something, even in a whisper. We just sit and eat together, and I realize that it feels nice having her sitting next to me. After lunch Skyla heads off down the corridor and I half-wonder whether I should follow, but she doesn't look back so I do my usual wandering. Today is a bit different, though. I see Jiggly Josh and Tall Matthew coming towards me.

"Hi, Billy," says Josh as he's approaching.

"Hi," I whisper.

"Great show-and-tell, by the way. You totally nailed it!" says Matthew.

"Thanks." My voice is getting a tiny bit louder with every word.

"I love jokes too," he adds. "How do you get a squirrel to like you?"

"Act like a nut?" I whisper, crossing my eyes and doing a little dance. He laughs and pats me on the back.

"You know it! We are meeting Alex in the Music Lounge, if you fancy it?"

"I m-m-m-might see you there," I mumble and they wave as they walk away.

Watching them I know that I won't go, not today anyway, but it doesn't matter because even though I'm still just wandering the corridors on my own it feels different now. I'm not invisible any more.

CHAPTER 11

Did you hear about the guy whose whole left side was cut off?
He's all right now.

The next day in history Blakemore holds up a piece of paper when Mrs Able isn't looking. It says:

EVERYONE FEEL SSSSSSORRY FOR BBBBBILLY PPPLIMPTON

Some of the kids look really mad at him but some of the others start laughing behind their hands. Skyla grabs the paper off him and rips it up.

"Skyla Norkins, is there any reason why you are tearing up school property?" Mrs Able is really nice but her strict voice is pretty scary; she goes really quiet when she's telling someone off, and it's way more effective than shouting.

"No, miss. Sorry."

"Well, don't let me see you doing that again."

When I turn back to Blakemore he has a new sign:

SKYLA STINKS

I wish I could grab it off him and rip it up for her. I think about Skyla looking after herself, eating her tea on her own at home while her mum lies in bed. In every lesson after that there's a new sign. I try to ignore them. I don't even want to read the words but I can't help myself.

TTTELL US A JJJJJOKE, BBBBBILLY

BBBBILLY CCCCAN'T EVEN SSSSPEAK

BBBBILLY PPPPLIMPTON
LOVES SSSSCABBY SKYLA

As I'm doing my lunchtime wandering Blakemore finds me and grabs me by the arm. He leads me down the corridor and whispers, "Don't say a word about this to anyone, Plimpton," then laughs to himself. "Ha, I forgot, you CAN'T say a word to anyone, can you?" then he shoves me into the boys' toilets and takes out his phone.

"Ya goin' to do a little performance, Billy. I know you love jokes, so don't worry, this'll be funny. It's like your first comedy show! YouTube'll blow up when it sees this." Then he presses record on his phone and points it at me.

I really don't know what he's going to make me do. I'm scared that he might make me strip or drink out of the toilet but then he says, "Ya just goin' to say the alphabet, Billy, that's all. When we get to the end you can go." He grins a horrible grin. "But remember we need you to say it nice and clearly. N-N-N-No hesitation."

I try and run but he grabs me and shoves me back. I have no chance, Blakemore is twice my size. I stand there hot and shaking. If I just wait it out and say nothing, he'll get bored before I do. "Don't make me wait, Billy," he growls, and then he gives me another shove in the stomach, this time hard enough to really hurt. I decide to give him what he wants, how bad can it be?

"A, B-B-B-B-B..."

"Oh no, Billy... Start again!"

It takes twenty-five minutes, inhaling the stench of boys' wee, him laughing at every letter. The pointlessness of starting back at "A" knowing that I will never make it to the end, but not being able to stop. The growing humiliation with every attempt. I only get as far as "D". Eventually he gets bored, shoves me into the door and wanders off. I feel exhausted and just want to go home and crawl into bed.

When I come out of school, Dad's waiting for me at the gates. He never picks me up so I know straight away that something's wrong. His face looks old and he's very still. At first I think it's because of me. I must have done something. My head starts swimming with thoughts and panic. Has he seen Blakemore's video? Then he bends down and holds my hands and looks at me right in the eyes.

"Granny Bread's in hospital, Bill. She's had a stroke."

I have no idea what a stroke is when Dad first says it. I know it's bad, though, because of *how* he says it. I don't say a word in the car and neither does he. Instead I count all the red cars I can see as we drive. There are fourteen. If I stop counting cars then my brain might start thinking about Granny Bread being ill. So I just keep counting. I google "stroke" on the iPad as soon as I get home.

A stroke is a serious life-threatening
medical condition that occurs when the
blood supply to part of the brain is cut off.

It doesn't make me feel any better. *Life threatening.*

Mum won't let me go to the hospital. "Not until we know how things are looking. I need to see how she is first," she says. She looks really tired too. I want to argue. To say that Granny Bread needs me. That I *have* to be there. But seeing Mum's sad face, as she picks up her handbag and turns towards the door, I decide not to.

Dad says I can go on the iPad until she gets back and so I get into my star onesie, flop on to the sofa next to Chloe and start watching my favourite comedians. It doesn't feel right though, watching people telling jokes when Granny Bread is so ill. As I'm staring blankly at the screen I remember Blakemore laughing at me, pointing his phone in my face. What if he's put it up? I check that Chloe isn't looking over my shoulder, but she's fixated on some pony cartoon, and so I start searching for the video, praying that it's not there. I look under his name and mine and then under everything else I can think of: *Stammering kid, stuttering alphabet, kid can't speak, funny stammerer, abc stutter.* I breathe a sigh of relief when nothing comes up. That's the last thing Mum needs to deal with right now, me going viral for being bullied. I sit there, fed up, and wonder what to watch. Eventually I decide on Granny Bread's favourite episode of *Blue Planet.* I just think about the Dumbo octopus and try to remember all the facts to tell Granny Bread when I see her. She'll be OK. She *has* to be OK. When it's over I go back to the start and press play again. Chloe gets really irritated when she looks at my screen.

"Why are you watching it again, Billy? You are so annoying."

"You're so annoying with your b-b-boring pony programmes," I shout, and then Dad comes in and tells her it's time for bed.

"What about him?" she whines.

"He's older than you."

"What about Granny Bread?"

"I will wake you up if anything happens."

"W-W-What do you mean by that?" I say. "You mean if she d-d-d..."

"ENOUGH! Thank you, Billy. Chloe, bed, now, please." She knows there's no point arguing.

Later, when I'm on my third viewing of *Blue Planet*, I hear Mum's car outside. I press pause and run out in my slippers to meet her. She looks even more tired and ushers me back into the house. When Dad hugs her she starts crying. I think that Granny Bread is definitely dead because of the crying and so I start crying too, but then she sobs, "She's OK. They think she's going to be fine. It was a small stroke."

I wish Mum would cry at things that make more sense! Why is she crying if Granny Bread's OK? Anyway, I wipe my eyes and give her a hug. She really looks like she needs one.

I'm allowed to visit Granny Bread the next day. The hospital smells funny. We have to put cold wet stuff on our hands on the way in and out. It makes me worry about germs; I don't want to touch anything. I start opening all the doors in the hospital with my elbows. Mum says I am a "strange fish" and then tells me off in the whispery angry voice that she uses on Chloe and me in supermarkets for using too much of the cold stuff.

"You just need one squirt, not ten!" she hisses. "Honestly, Billy!"

There's an old man in the bed next to Granny Bread who keeps groaning really loudly and saying, "Help me." Mum goes and finds a nurse to look after him but he keeps saying it even after the nurse has been to see him. It's a bit scary. He looks right at me when he says it. I really want to help him, but I don't know how. Then Chloe gets really scared and starts crying. So Mum takes her out.

"You stay with Granny Bread, Billy. I'll just take Chloe for some fresh air."

I hope Chloe doesn't come back. That suits me. I want it to just be me and Granny Bread. I don't want to leave her, even though she's tired and falls in and out of sleep as I'm talking to her. She looks really old, lying in her hospital gown with a plastic tag wrapped around her wrinkly wrist. Her face is pale and she has trouble talking and dribbles from one side of her mouth. It makes me feel a bit awkward seeing the dribble. Mum wipes it with a handkerchief, and so when she and Chloe have gone I do the same. It feels weird at first but then I just get used to it.

Granny Bread's voice is all weak and slurry and it's hard to understand what she's saying, at first.

"Tell mmee a jjjjjoke, Billly," she slurs.

"Guess who I saw yesterday, Granny Bread?"

"Who?"

"Everyone I looked at!"

I can feel her laughing and her eyes get full of tears. I start crying then, out of nowhere, tears just pop out of my eyes as I'm holding her hand and feeling her shaking with laughter. She looks at me and squeezes my hand hard.

"I'm not going anywhere, Billy. Wipe away those tears. You have got more jokes left to tell me yet, don't you worry. Talk to me, Billy."

Then she stops talking and just listens, still holding my hand. I tell her about school and then talk about things I know she likes. I tell her again and again about the octopus on *Blue Planet*. I tell her facts about how deep in the sea it lives and how rare it is. How they live so deep that no one ever sees them.

I remember her saying once, "It seems a shame that they don't come up to the surface. People would love to see them." I remember thinking that people would probably scream or kill them if they popped up at the seaside. People don't like things that are too different. Not in my experience anyway.

It's hard talking to someone who doesn't talk back. When I run out of things to say I read to her from the book on her table by the bed. It has a little cottage on the front surrounded by flowers. When I finish the chapter I tell her some more jokes. She is too tired to laugh but she closes her eyes and squeezes my hand at every punchline.

Chloe falls asleep in the car on the way home and I pretend to sleep too. Sometimes when I want to hear what Mum and Dad will talk about I do this. I have got the breathing just right. Mum used to know when I was faking and I figured out it was because of the breath. Now I can trick her every time. They still talk in whispers in the car but I can hear what they're saying. They say that Granny Bread might have to go into a care home when she comes out of the hospital.

"The nurses said that there is a possibility she will need help with everything. Like going to the toilet and eating her dinner," Mum says. She sounds really worried.

"Well, let's wait and see," Dad says. "She's a trooper, she might be on her feet in no time."

"They said if someone had been with her then the stroke might not have been so bad, she could have got to hospital quicker. I feel so guilty, Ian."

I imagine Granny Bread on her own in her flat

needing help and it makes my throat hurt, so as soon as I pretend to wake up I tell Mum that she can come to our house, have my room, and I'll share with Chloe.

"Then I can look after her," I say.

Mum laughs and says, "That's a lovely thought, sweetie, but she can't stay with us."

"W-W-W-Why not?" I feel like she isn't really listening to me.

"Because, Billy, we have one toilet, which is upstairs. She could barely use the stairs before this happened. I don't think the stroke's going to have improved things, do you?" She's angry now and her face looks red and blotchy. She looks like she might cry and I remember then that Granny Bread is actually *her* mum.

Sometimes it's hard to remember that, I just think she's mine. My Granny Bread. I think about how I'd feel if this was happening to Mum. If I was about to put her into a home with groaning men and a bad smell. If I had to wipe dribble from the corner of *her* mouth. Then my throat goes all tight so I stop thinking about it.

"S-S-Sorry, Mum."

"It's OK, sweetie. I know it's hard for you. She loves

you so much, you know that, don't you? You and your jokes brighten up her life."

"Yeah. I know," I say, and I mean it. I remember Granny Bread sitting on her flowery sofa and think about my pinky promise to her.

CHAPTER 12

What do you call a man trapped in a paper bag?
Russell.

Most lunchtimes, after our pizza, chips, apple juice and yoghurt (me and Skyla have the same thing every day now) I sneak into the theatre and sit in the empty seats. Once she came with me but she didn't really understand what we were doing there.

"You just sit here?"

"Yep."

"Why?" she asked.

"I l-like looking at the stage."

"I'm not sure why I stick up for you sometimes, Billy!" she said. Then she punched me lightly on the arm and slung her bag over her shoulder and walked off towards the door. Then she stopped and called back to me.

"Maybe you should get *on* the stage one day, you weirdo! See you in form class, Bilbo."

That's what gave me the idea.

When the theatre's busy, with people singing or dancing on the stage, I either watch them through the little window or go and find somewhere quiet to read. I try to avoid anywhere I might have to speak. The library's OK at lunchtime, or there is a good reading spot under the stairwell where no one can see me. Sometimes I still wander around looking in the windows of the art rooms for Skyla but I can never find her. She won't tell me where she goes. "None of your business! Anyway if we spend too much time together people will start talking about us, even more than they already do."

It's nice to have one person to talk to while I eat my lunch. It's actually quite hard being quiet all the time in lessons, especially when I know the answers but don't want to say them out loud. So by lunchtime I am ready to talk to someone. I've even started trying out some of my jokes on her, in my proper voice too, not just a whisper any more. She's a good audience, but not as good as Granny Bread; she can always spot my jokes coming whereas Granny Bread never can.

"I l-l-l-learned something interesting today, Skyla."

"Oh, here we go... What?" she says, rolling her eyes.

"Do you know why b-birds fly to warmer countries in winter?"

"So they don't freeze?"

"No, because it's easier than walking!"

She kind of snorts and then packs up her tray.

"Will you ever run out of jokes?"

"N-N-N-NEVER!" I say loudly and do a massive evil laugh, "*Mua ha ha ha ha!*" and rub my hands together like a villain. She laughs at this and picks up her tray and heads out of the dinner hall.

Today my lunchtime plan is to go to the theatre and actually stand on the stage. So I can feel it. I have been too nervous so far. Scared of the empty rows staring back at me silently. I get as far as the little steps leading up to the side of the stage, but each time I try to step up my heart starts thumping and my feet won't move. Every day I go a tiny bit further than the day before and I have now somehow finally made it to the last step. With only one more step to go, today's the day. I'm excited.

I'm going to tell Skyla after I have done it. I finish my lunch super fast and make my way out of the dinner hall. William Blakemore's standing in the corridor, leaning against the wall, like he's been waiting for me. This is now normal, he is like my very own stalker. It's usually after lunch, but sometimes he mixes it up, surprises me outside the library or between lessons. As bullies go he's a pretty good one. Committed.

He grabs me by the shoulders, squeezes hard, and says in his hideous voice, "Say 'Excuse me, Lord William'."

Most of the time there's someone to stick up for me if they see him anywhere near me, which is nice. Elsie and Yasmin always tell him to leave me alone. After the show-and-tell they told me that they think I'm "cute", and obviously I've always got Skyla. Last week she even slapped him in the face when he was throwing my bag around after IT. She got a detention. I wish I had the guts to slap him in the face. Blakemore isn't very nice to Skyla either. He says horrible things about her family. Today I look around and she's nowhere to be seen, no one is, so I guess I have no other choice and start speaking.

"Excuuuse m-m-m-me, L-L-L-Lord Wiiilliam."

When I've finally got to the end of the humiliating sentence I try to squeeze past him. He pretends to be laughing too much to get out of the way and slaps me on the back, hard, grabs me again, and says, "You are soooo funny. Thanks, Billy. Thanks!" He's holding me tight on the shoulders now, his thumbs digging into my collarbones. I know that he isn't going to let me go. "Now, w-w-w-what do ya' wanna say next, eh, B-B-B-B-B-Bill?" he sneers.

As he's thinking about what to make me say, he takes one hand away from my shoulder to scratch his head.

This is it, my chance. Who do I want to be in this moment? The boy who stays and takes it, again. Or the boy who does something about it.

I take my moment, duck to get out of his grasp and run. I'm not much of a runner, but William Blakemore's *terrible* at running, I have seen him in PE, so I know I can get away. It doesn't stop him from trying, though. He's not far behind me either. As I run down the corridor, heart pounding and eyes bulging, on my left I see an open door, I duck in and slam it behind me.

I close my eyes, and take big deep breaths in and out, when a voice says, "Billy! Well, that's a way to make an entrance. I'm glad you're so keen to join us! Come in! Come in!" It's Mr Osho's Music Lounge. I'd forgotten all about it! "Perfect timing," he continues. "I've just finished my marking and am looking for an opponent. Do you fancy a game? We need a catch-up anyway, don't we?"

I nod and look around the room. There's some mellow music playing and a few kids are sitting around on beanbags, chatting. Tall Matthew, Jiggly Josh and Alex are there too, sitting around a low table playing a really complicated game with orcs and warlords in it. When they look up and see me they all wave. It looks so peaceful. Safe. I instantly forget all about William Blakemore.

Mr Osho sits at a table with a big carved wooden board on it that has little stones in each section. "This is Miles Davis," he says, gesturing to the music in the air. "You ever heard of Miles Davis?"

Mr Osho has asked to look in my notebook but I don't know what to write in it. I can't exactly write: *GET RID OF WILLIAM BLAKEMORE*, can I? I know that if I *ever* tell on Blakemore, my life will get much worse. So the pages are all blank. Mr Osho always looks a bit sad when he sees them. When he asks if I'm OK I just nod and whisper that I'm fine. I can't tell him that since the day of the ME ME speech I have actually been completely silent, to everyone apart from Skyla. I can't tell him that the only time that I speak in more than a whisper is when William Blakemore forces me to.

I realize, as Mr Osho waits for me to answer with his kind, worried face, that I want to talk to him, in more than a whisper. I don't have to tell him about Blakemore, do I? I can just "chat".

"M-M-M-My granny likes M-M-M-Miles D-D-D-D-Davis," I reply. Hearing my voice talk about Granny Bread feels strange. I really hope that I'm not going too red. Imagining Granny Bread in her hot little crowded room, listening to Miles Davis on cassette, and imagining her now in her hospital bed makes my throat get tight.

Mr Osho puts his hand on my shoulder and says, "Well, your granny must be very special." Then he points to a game and says, "Do you know how to play Mancala?" I'm so pleased he doesn't ask me anything more about her. I smile and shake my head.

He got the wooden board when he was a kid, visiting his grandparents in Nigeria; he says that his grandad carved it for him. The way he strokes the smooth wood makes me think it must be very precious, and I wonder if his grandad is still alive but I don't ask.

"The little stones are actually seed pods from a tree," he says. "Shake it and you can hear a little seed inside." I keep shaking it next to my ear. They feel really nice. Smooth.

He beats me four times but then I beat him once.

"You still into jokes, Billy?" he says as we are collecting all the little stones up for a final round.

"Not so much," I say.

"Really?"

"I'm m-m-more into books at the m-m-moment," I say, setting up the perfect joke, as we start up the game.

"What are you reading?"

"I'm reading a book on anti-g-g-g-gravity, sir. It's so brilliant ... I can't put it down." Then I mime not being able to put something down because it keeps floating away. "Get it, sir? A b-b-b-book on anti-gravity that I l-l-literally can't put down!"

At this he laughs so hard and hits the table with his hand. I get a bit embarrassed that everyone's looking at us. I think Mr Osho might be the best audience member ever, maybe even as good as Granny Bread. I'm definitely going to try out more jokes on him.

"You are destined for a life on the stage, Billy," he says as he moves one of his stones.

"H-H-Hardly, sir. You c-c-can't get up onstage if you caan't even s-speak p-properly." I'm surprised when I say this, it feels too honest, but there's something about Mr Osho that makes me want to talk to him, like it's OK to be myself.

"Why on earth not?" he says. "Anyway you do speak 'properly', just a bit different. I tell you what, there's nothing wrong with being unusual, especially as a performer. Creative people are *meant* to be different to the rest. Did you know Elvis had a stammer?"

"No!"

"Yes, and Ed Sheeran."

"I n-never knew that," I say.

"Don't let it stop you from doing anything you want to, Billy."

When the bell goes I pack away and head back to form room. I sit in my usual spot next to Alex. I'm feeling more confident after my chat with Mr Osho and so I decide to go for it.

"W-W-W-What were you guys playing?" I ask, trying to sound casual.

"It's called Castle Panic," he says. "It's awesome."

Then Josh says from over my shoulder, "We can teach you if you like?"

"Y-Y-Yeah, that w-would be good," I say. I look up and see Skyla watching me with a little smile on her face, and then just behind her Blakemore with a very different smile on his.

CHAPTER 13

What party game do fish like to play?
Salmon Says.

Granny Bread moved into The Oaks care home this week. On Sunday she's "too weak" to come to us for lunch, like she normally does, so after football (we lose) we go to see her in her new room. It's even hotter than her flat. All of her things are around but it's much smaller than the flat so it's pretty cramped.

The Oaks is a long, low red-brick building and nearly everyone there is either in bed or in a wheelchair. I see a few people in a big room asleep in chairs and wonder if they're dead. It feels like another hospital. It smells horrid. Like cooking and rot. The only good thing about The Oaks care home is that I can walk there from our house on my own, so I don't need to get a lift from Mum. After the visit I walk home on my own so that I can time it. It takes eight minutes exactly.

I'm going to go and see her and tell her a new joke every day.

I think she's scared in The Oaks. She looks scared. She looked at me just like the man in the hospital did when he said, "Help me." The way she looked at me made me want to run away and hide under my duvet. It's scaring me even thinking about it now. I'd better change the subject. Like Mum says when I'm worrying, "Just think of something else. Change the channel, Bill!"

Sometimes my brain doesn't listen when I try to change the subject, though. It just keeps flicking it back over to the worry channel. I don't know what I'm meant to do then. Anyway, here goes, I'm changing the channel...

I had my speech appointment with Sue on Friday. After we told her all about my show-and-tell and then played some games with the Smoothies, she says she thinks that I'm ready to tackle some "big challenges". She wants to talk to me on the phone every Wednesday until my next appointment to start "fighting the fear". As I'm nodding my head I'm already thinking that I might ignore her call. Phones are the worst.

When we're leaving she gives us a DVD of a documentary. She says it's "inspiring". We watch it after tea. It's all about this stammer school that people go to and stay at for two weeks. They're not allowed to talk to anyone they know for the whole time. They do things with straps around their tummies and then go and meet a hundred strangers in the street and ask them questions like, "Do you know the time?" and, "Can you tell me where the museum is?" even though they already know the answers. It looks terrifying. No one even mentions the disgusting tea.

Everyone on the programme has stammers worse than mine! I have never seen so many people all stammering at the same time. Some people have even weirder ones than me. One woman sounds like a cat crying every time she speaks. Another guy gets so stuck he looks like he's having a fit. I feel really sorry for them and I start to like my singing stammer a bit more.

At the end they have to get on to a box in a town centre and shout things to people. They all do it, and they don't get stuck much at all. The guy who looked like he was fitting even tells a joke! He doesn't stammer once. It's pretty amazing. When I turn to Mum as the credits come up, she's crying her eyes out, shaking and making little noises like a hamster. Then I look at Dad and he's crying too!

Dad *never* cries. Mum always laughs at him saying that he is made of stone because he didn't cry on their wedding day or when me and Chloe were born. He says that he was *happy* so why would he cry? That makes sense, if you ask me.

So I know that he's not happy at the end of the documentary but I don't understand why he's so *sad*.

"They did really well, Dad. Why are you both crying?" I ask.

"Yes, Billy, they did really well. It's just a bit much for your mum and me, that's all. Sorry, son," he answers, wiping his eyes.

Then Mum hugs me really tight for ages. "It's just amazing watching people overcome their fears. How strong they can be. It's beautiful, isn't it?"

I can't really answer, as she's holding me so tight, but I know what she means. I know that I want to be like the people on the documentary. Not to cheat and use signs, or whisper, or tap. I want to make Mum and Dad feel like this about me.

I just nod into her armpit and my eyes start going

funny. Then she wipes her face with her sleeve and holds my face in her hands and makes my cheeks feel all squashy. "You are such an incredible boy. It's time for bed."

I lie awake for ages. Thinking about it. Maybe this is what I have to do next, this can be part of my plan. Number one on the list of Ways to Get Rid of My Stammer. As I write the new list, that has only one thing on it, I realize that there is nothing else to write; I have tried and failed at everything else. This is it, my last chance. I look up to the sky.

"Is this the magic cure that I have been waiting for?" I get a shiver down my spine and pin up the list on to the middle of the board:

1. Go on the stammer course

I sneak downstairs, so slowly, one step at a time. I am pretty sure I can hear my heart beating. I try not to even breathe. I get my iPad out of the drawer in the hall, where Mum keeps it. When the drawer squeaks as I slide the wood back I think Mum and Dad must have heard me. I freeze. Wait. Listen hard – nothing. Halfway up the stairs I make a mad dash, taking them two at a time, and manage to get back up to my room without them hearing. I find the stammer school website straight away.

The next course is starting in a month! This is it. It's actually going to happen. I will be the one standing on that box telling a joke. Just like Granny Bread wanted me to, just like I pinky promised her. When I start typing the email I begin to feel a bit giddy, imagining life without my stammer.

Dear Stammer School,

My name is Billy Plimpton and I have a stammer. A *really* bad one. I am eleven years old. (I will be twelve in twenty-six days!) I just watched your DVD and I REALLY, REALLY want to come and do the next course.

Please send me the address and price and I'll bring the money with me.

I can't wait!

Yours sincerely,

Billy Plimpton

That night I dream I'm standing on stage at school between the velvet curtains telling jokes, and I don't get stuck once.

CHAPTER 14

What did the drummer name his two daughters?
Anna one, Anna two.

I go to Mr Osho's Music Lounge every day now. I've got a whole new routine that has no space in it for wandering around on my own. After lunch with Skyla, I run past the theatre, trying desperately to avoid the fist of Blakemore, and when it's empty, I dash in and straight up on to the stage. The first time I walked into the middle I wasn't even nervous any more, I just ran in and straight up the little stairs. I didn't quite know what to do when I got up there but when I turned to face the empty seats it felt great. I took a great big breath in and whispered, "Good evening, ladies and gentlemen," and imagined them all smiling back up at me. Then I carried on in a slightly bigger voice, "My name is B-B-Billy Plimpton. Just with the one 'B'." Some imaginary laughter and then louder again. "I would tell you a j-joke about herbs and f-f-f-fish but this isn't the thyme or plaice."

I imagine how people would laugh. Mr Osho slapping his hand down on his thigh, Skyla snorting or Granny Bread with her head back and eyes closed. I would love for them to see me up here. I've not had the guts to tell Skyla to come yet, I keep trying every lunch but I wimp out. I felt pretty proud of myself for even getting up on the stage, even though no one was in the audience. It's funny how sometimes things seem so scary at first. Then they change. In a moment. Like in my bedroom in the darkness, there's a monster, hunched up and staring. In the light it's my dressing gown, cosy and warm. The stage is more like my dressing gown now; I can see it in a different light.

Yesterday lunchtime I ran in without checking first and the stage was full of Year Nines rehearsing in ballet tutus. I flung the door open and was halfway down the aisle before I even noticed them. They all stopped what they were doing and stared at me. A thin teacher with a beaky-looking face said, "Can we help you?"

I raised my arms above my head, did my best pirouette and ran back out again to the sound of them all laughing and the thin beaky teacher shushing them. I headed straight to the Music Lounge like I do every day now, once I'm finished telling jokes to no one.

I've already learned loads of new games at the Music Lounge and listened to Ella Fitzgerald, Louis Armstrong and Art Blakey. Miles Davis is still my favourite. They are all jazz singers and musicians. Jazz drumming is insane. It's so fast.

When I tell Mr Osho that I have been practising jazz beats he looks at the regulars and says, "Right, boys, you set up the game. Billy, you come with me, kiddo," and gestures for me to follow him. As we walk down the corridor he says, "Every October we set the Music Lounge up into a rehearsal room. I was going to wait until the drums were set up in there but the minute you mentioned jazz drumming, that was it. I can't watch you tap-tap-tapping with those pencils any more. It's time to drum, Billy Plimpton."

"Where are we going, sir?"

"Sixth form building. Music studio."

"Am I allowed?"

"You are if you're with me, kid. But you have to tell the scary sixth formers to get out, OK?!"

"No way!" I say, laughing. "You know that I've never actually p-p-played on a proper kit, sir?"

"Why do you think we are doing this? I've seen you tapping, that rhythm needs to come out! If it stays inside much longer you might pop!"

"That's what my mum says."

"What? That you're going to pop?!"

"That I've got too much going on in my b-b-brain and it *looks* like I might pop."

"There's definitely lots going on up there, kid."

"Th-that's why I stammer. My brain is too full up. That's what my speech therapist s-s-says. Other people, when their b-brain gets too full, get stressed or c-can't sleep or get tummy aches. I stammer."

"That makes sense. Even more reason to let some of it out on the drums, then, eh?"

"What happens to you, sir, when your brain gets too full?"

"Ooh, good question. I bite my nails, and once when it got REALLY full, when I was a little bit older than you, my hair started falling out," he says as we arrive at the top building.

"Really? Were you bald?" I ask.

"No, it was just in patches and it all grew back eventually, but not a good thing to happen at secondary school, as you can imagine, and I was already a bit of an outsider, so that made things worse."

"That's rubbish, sir," I say, wondering if I would rather be bald than have a stammer.

There is a free drum kit when we get there and Mr Osho claps his hands together. "Look at that, you don't even have to get rid of anyone! Right, Billy, show me what you've got."

It's so much harder with proper sticks and drums than with pencils and I keep getting easy beats that I can do on my knees totally wrong on the drum kit.

"It's harder in real life, isn't it?" Mr Osho says.

"Much!" I say, rubbing my hands.

"But you are way better than if you were starting from scratch, you have the rhythm. You just have to make sure that your brain's not going too fast for your body. Let me show you the easiest 4/4 beat. You can play this to most things." He takes the sticks and sits at the drums and slowly breaks down what each hand and foot is doing.

"Right, now give it a go, but you have to go slowly. You can't be in a rush with drumming, you have to find a beat that you can keep."

I start a slow four beat with my right hand and then add in my left on every three and then when that is steady add in the kick drum on the one. It actually sounds like a drum beat!

"Keep going!" Mr Osho says, picking up a bass guitar and plucking a few strings in time to the drums. I feel a bit giddy, like I might start laughing, and try to go a bit faster, and that's when I mess up. But Mr Osho doesn't focus on the end. He focuses on what came before it. "Thats it! You did it. Feel good?"

"Amazing!" I say, starting up the beat again and instantly losing it.

"Well, now you know the feel of it, practise this with your pencils and adding your foot in, and you can use the kit in the Music Lounge soon enough."

"Thanks, sir."

"My absolute pleasure, Billy."

As we head back to the Music Lounge, he says, "I know that you've not wanted to write anything down in your book, but you know you can chat to me whenever you want, don't you?"

"Yes, sir. Sorry, sir, do you want the b-b-b-book back?"

"Of course not. You might want to write in it one

day, let some of the stuff in that full brain out on to the page!"

"I write loads at home, sir."

"Like what?"

"Lists and s-s-stuff. Stupid things, like what annoys my sister and jokes, b-b-but sometimes I write about my stammer."

"What do you write?"

"Just how to get rid of it and ways to stay invisible, sir. Stuff like that."

"Do you feel like the stammer is the only thing getting in your way?"

"Y-Y-Yeah. I'm g-g-going to get rid of it, sir," I say, thinking about the course.

"Well, I'm glad you are feeling positive about it, Billy. But, you know, even if you can't get rid of it, it's only *one* thing about you. There is *so* much more to you than that. Give me that notebook." I hand it over, not knowing where this is going.

"OK, so you like lists, Billy?" he asks. I nod. "Well if someone asked me to write a list about you, this is what I would write."

He stops walking, takes a pen from his pocket, rests the notebook on his knee and starts writing:

THINGS I KNOW ABOUT
BILLY PLIMPTON

1. He is FUNNY . . . VERY FUNNY.
2. He is not so bad on the drums either.
3. He is a good student.
4. He comes to the Music Lounge
   every day.
5. He loves his granny.
6. I regularly beat him at Mancala.

Then he leaves this huge gap and at the bottom of the
page in tiny writing puts:

Oh, yes, and he also has a stammer.

It makes me smile as he hands over the notebook. We
keep walking and I hold it tightly in my hands.

"Maybe rather than focusing on getting rid of your
stammer, you could try and see yourself the way that
other people see you?"

"Not everyone is as nice as you, sir," I say, picturing
what Blakemore would do to me if he ever found the
notebook.

When we get back to the Music Lounge the boys

are halfway through a game of Geist Blitz. I have learned so many new games.

My new favourites are Rubik's Race, Forbidden Island and last week Mr Osho taught us to play poker! At first I was terrible at bluffing. Bluffing is where you pretend you have good cards when you have got bad ones, or the other way round. Alex, Matthew, Josh and Mr Osho laughed at me loads when I pumped my fist in the air and did a little dance as I was dealt two aces. We bet with pieces of Lego. Mr Osho says it's even better to bet with Smarties, when you can eat them at the end, but we don't have Smarties. Reds are worth one, blues two, and whites are worth five. After he taught us the rules he went to change the record and we carried on. He plays his music on a little record player that folds up into a suitcase with a handle. It's pretty awesome. He calls the records "vinyl".

There are some Year Nine girls who go when it's raining, and a few Year Eights who just sit on the beanbags, but me, Matthew, Josh and Alex go every day. We are "the regulars". That's what Mr Osho calls us. I go over and join in with whatever game "the regulars" are setting up. They don't seem to mind me hanging around.

"Hey, Billy."

"What's it t-t-t-today?"

"Castle Panic!" says Matthew, laying out the pieces.

"I've got to leave early," I say casually, setting myself up. "I've got the dentist l-l-later."

"I hate the dentist," frowns Josh. "He always puts that horrible stuff on my teeth."

"I'm amazed you can sit still enough, Josh, to even go to the dentist!" laughs Matthew and does an impression of him jiggling around with his mouth wide open.

"Well, I bet you are too big for the chair," says Josh.

Matthew is six feet tall already. I'm only just five feet, so you can imagine how ridiculous we look next to each other. He can pick me up from under my armpits. He says he wants to use me as a weight to build up his biceps. He has a growth thing, it's got a funny name, something syndrome. That's why he's so tall. He'll probably have problems with his bones when he is older. He told me about it when we were packing a game up. I think he should be a basketball player, he can nearly do a slam dunk already. He showed me in PE.

"You missing English?" Alex asks.

"Yeah, I've got to leave after form class," I say. "My appointment's at TOOTH HURTY. Get it?! Two-thirty. TOOTH HURTY," and with that they all groan and Josh throws a game piece at me which I catch and pretend to eat.

Josh is nearly as small as me. He has black hair and really blue eyes. He kind of looks like a wolf. He is the one who never stops moving. When we play games, and he is waiting for his turn, he folds bits of paper or fidgets with a little cube he has in his pocket. He's always jiggling because he has something called ADHD, which means he can't sit still. He takes pills for it, but he still jiggles. In form class, when I'm drumming with pencils and he's jiggling, Alex says it looks like we are listening to our own imaginary music.

After Alex's speech about his hearing aid, I had been worried about whether he'd be able to lip read me. I'd avoided talking to him, but when we started playing games in the Music Lounge I thought I'd better check. I got up the courage to ask if he could understand what I was saying, and he said he could lip read me fine and didn't understand what the fuss was about.

He said, "You can't speak and I can't hear. We're

the perfect match!" That made me feel really good. I know he wasn't lying too, because he *always* laughs at my jokes. He laughs all the time actually. He said once as he was laughing, "Billy, you know, you're even funnier when you're just being you, messing about, even more than when you're telling jokes!"

I didn't even know what I had done that was so funny, but it was a nice thing to say. Mr Osho says that all together we are "a right motley crew". Whatever that means!

What Alex said reminds me of the comedian me and Granny Bread saw on the telly. Maybe, after I've been on the course I shouldn't just tell "jokes"; maybe I should find a way to be a bit more me. Some comedians tell stories and some do physical comedy. I just need to think of something that makes me unique.

When I visit Granny Bread at The Oaks after school, I try telling a funny story about Chloe on an imaginary pony. I gallop around the tiny room, but she dozes off halfway through so it doesn't really work. When she wakes up I re-enact my worst moment from Sunday's match. I stand in the middle of the room and, in slow motion with commentary, act out the ball hitting me on the head and then bouncing up on to the top post, coming back down and hitting me again before bouncing off into the net and scoring the other team their eighteenth goal of the match. She laughs and calls me "a card", whatever that means. I'm not sure if storytelling comedy is for me. I think she laughs more at my one-liners.

I stick Mr Osho's list up on my pinboard when I get in, but I hide it behind the others. It's a bit embarrassing to look at it, for some reason. Maybe because I just don't believe that it's true, but it feels good pinning it up there. Even though I can't see it, I know it's there. I'm still waiting to hear from the stammer school, I can't quite believe that by Christmas my stammer will be gone. I'll be able to do *anything*.

CHAPTER 15

**What do you get when you run behind a car?
Exhausted.**

At the end of the race, running across the boggy field
towards the looming school, my cheeks are stinging
and my chest is screaming at me to stop. I'm third
from the back. Behind Elsie and just in front of Skyla.
I HATE cross-country. I can just about see Alex
ahead but everyone else is way out in front. So I have
no choice. I just keep going.

After the race we are all paired with a Year Twelve
who will tell us our time and then take us to the
water fountains to fill our bottles. They're all doing
a "sports leaders" course for PE and have to fill in
questionnaires and do warm-ups with us. My Year
Twelve is called Ellie and is nearly as tall as Matthew!

She has really curly red hair and spots on her face that I try not to look at. I just stare at her lace-up shoes and feel my ears get hot.

On the way down the corridor, I hear a familiar sound.

Bbrrm tat, Bbrrm bbrrmm tattat.
Bbrrm tat, Bbrrm bbrrmm tattat.
Bbrrm tat, Bbrrm bbrrmm tattat.

It's a 4/4 drum beat in a kind of marching rhythm.

So far on our journey down the corridor, past all the science labs and textile rooms, I've avoided saying anything to Ellie. Talking to bigger kids is the absolute worst. Especially total strangers. I'm OK now chatting to Skyla, Alex, Josh, Matthew and Mr Osho. I have even answered some questions in maths in my whispery voice, but with Ellie I feel really nervous. I'm using my classic trick of pretending to be shy. It isn't hard to fake it. I'm sure I'm bright red. Ellie asks me loads of questions.

"Did you enjoy the race?"

"It's a big school, isn't it?"

"Do you like science?"

She talks like grown-ups do, even though she is technically still a kid. I want to look at her but I keep my eyes fixed on her feet. I nod at her questions and try to smile. But now listening to the drums, this is more important. I HAVE to speak!

I can feel my heart thumping in my chest; hear it loud in my ears. My mouth is dry as I take a big breath in, put my hand on my tummy like Sue makes me, and then just as I'm about to go for it, I stop. I can't do it. But the drums keep going.

Brrmm tattat, tattat, rrrrm tat.

However hard I try I can't ignore them.

Brrmm tattat, tattat, rrrrm tat.

It sounds like they are getting louder. Then it just happens. "Is someone playing the drums?" I say. *I said it! I actually said it! I didn't even stammer.*

I think I must look quite surprised as Ellie kind of smiles at me then, like she knows. "Yeah, I think they are setting up in the Music Lounge."

"I g-g-go to the Music Lounge!" I say as though it's the best thing ever.

"Shall we go and check it out?" she asks.

After that it's much easier to talk to Ellie. I answer her questionnaire as we make our way to the sound of the drumming. She is a Waiter. I even tell her a joke as we head up the stairs.

"I don't trust s-s-stairs," I say in my most suspicious voice. "They are always *up* t-t-t-to s-s-s-something."

"You're funny!" she says, and she doesn't seem to notice my stutter at all.

One half of the Music Lounge is being set up like a studio. It looks amazing. There are some kids in there who are playing a song that they have written themselves! It's about breaking things, I think, but it's quite hard to understand. The drummer keeps getting stuck on the same bit again and again. I'm desperate to go in and play for Ellie. I would love to play on a proper kit, and I'm sure I can play the beat that the boy's getting wrong. But she says we should get back, "before they send out a search party".

As we're leaving, Ellie says, "They're practising for the talent show, I think."

"T-T-Talent sh-show?"

"It's huge. Every December in the theatre. Last year it was on the local news!"

When the bell goes she waves me off at the changing room and shouts, "Maybe I will get to hear you drumming one day, they have an open rehearsal for the talent show soon. I'll be there."

On the way back to class, I imagine Ellie in the audience while I'm on the stage, but I'm not drumming, I'm telling jokes. I don't know why that popped into my brain, it makes me feel a bit dizzy thinking about it, so I try to change the channel. It keeps turning back, though, putting new thoughts in. If I've been on the course and my stammer's gone maybe I *could* get up on the stage in front of a real audience instead of always having to imagine it.

On my way to The Oaks after school I remember my pinky promise to Granny Bread, that I would do a show just for her. Imagine if I did a show just for her and three hundred other people too! How proud she would be. She needs cheering up more than anything since the stroke. I know that I want to be able to do the talent show for her more than anything in the world.

When I walk in I see her on her flowery sofa in front of *Countdown*. Next to her sits a lady who looks even older than she is. She has a full face of make-up and a fancy hat on her head as though she is about to go to a party, not just sit and watch *Countdown* in an old people's home. She looks so old and there is something weird about her, scary. Like a haunted skeleton in fancy dress. There's a metal walking frame next to the sofa and a plate full of biscuits on the table.

"This is Mrs Gibbens, Billy." Granny Bread says My new neighbour." Mrs Gibbens looks up and waves a bony hand at me and then tries to get out of the sofa.

"Help her up, Billy. Once she's in she can't get out, can you, love?" I put out my arm and feel Mrs Gibbens's frail, wrinkly hand grab on. I try not to shudder as she touches me. Eventually she manages to get up, hold on to the walking frame and slowly make her way towards the door. Then she stops halfway and says,

"Scraggles!" in a voice that sounds as wrinkly and haunted as her flesh. Granny Bread picks up what looks like a photograph of a dog from next to the biscuits and presses it into Mrs Gibbens's hand.

"Here he is, dear. Don't worry. Here he is."

"Oh, Scraggles, my sweet boy," Mrs Gibbens says, clinging on to the picture and then continuing her slow walk to the door.

When she's gone Granny Bread whispers, "Terribly sad woman. Completely alone in the world."

I look down the corridor and see her sad frail body disappear into the next door along. I feel a shiver run down my spine. Mrs Gibbens scares me.

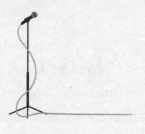

CHAPTER 16

What did the tree say to the bully?
Leaf me alone.

No response from the stammer school yet. Mum keeps asking me why I'm checking my emails so much. I lie and tell her I've entered a competition. I don't know why, but I don't want her to know. Not yet. I want it to be a surprise.

I started practising my set in the mirror straight away (a set is what comedians call the list of jokes they will do). I dream about telling my jokes onstage every night now. Sometimes it doesn't work out so well and I wake up crying, all sweaty, and have to go and cuddle Mum. But the good dreams when it *does* work, when I *can* speak, make me feel so happy.

The theatre at school is now covered in posters.

B.G.T

Bannerdale's Got Talent!

Have you got a talent?
Are you a singer, dancer,
magician, musician or performer?
We need you!

7.30 p.m. Thursday December 17th
Sign up at the school office to book
your moment in the spotlight.

Before maths I go straight to the school office to look at the sign-up sheet. There are four names already on it. I hope it doesn't get full before I've been on the stammer course. As I'm about to walk away, a little voice whispers in my head, *Do it!* I laugh to myself. I can't sign up before I have fixed my stammer, can I? Then I tell myself that the course starts in two weeks, I will go on it and then everything will be fine. I have all my jokes ready. What could go wrong?

I feel a surge of excitement as I pick up the pen

and quickly put my name on the list before I chicken out. The office lady, who's sitting at her desk eating a biscuit, and has a hairy mole on her face, looks at me and smiles.

"Brave boy!" she says, spitting out crumbs, and I grin back. I feel like a different person, like I can do anything.

I'm pretty relaxed in my maths exam too, apart from all the shushing before it starts. This is the last one before they move us into sets. I hate shushing. Some of the girls are being really intense, saying things like, "This is SOOO important. It could change the path of your life." I think that's a bit much, it's only a maths test.

I quite like exams. Not that I would ever say that to anyone. I like the quiet. The sound of everyone's pens scratching away at the paper. Everyone doing the same thing. It's really simple.

Mum says that I'm very "black and white", that I like everything to be clear. Good/Bad. Right/Wrong. I think she's right. That's why I like lists and plans and knowing what's going to happen. That's also why I'm pretty good at maths. There is always a right and wrong answer. No in between.

I finish the test with loads of time to spare. Even

after checking all of the questions twice. We're allowed to read our independent reading books when we finish but I don't. I watch William Blakemore instead. He looks really sad. He's not so good at maths. I like watching him when he doesn't know. When he's being real. Not howling with laughter or wrestling with someone. When he looks like a little kid and not a bully. Last week I saw him in the big supermarket on the edge of town with his mum. They were choosing cereal. I secretly watched him from the cat food aisle. She told him to get some Shreddies and when he took them off the shelf his arm knocked another packet on to the floor.

"Can't you do ANYTHING right?" she snapped at him, as she snatched the cereal out of his hand and headed off down the aisle with the trolley. He paused for a moment looking at the box on the floor, wondering whether to pick it up.

"WILLIAM!" his mother barked from over her shoulder, and with that he kicked the fallen box and shuffled after her.

As I was staring over at the Shreddies my mum came and asked really loud, "What on earth are you doing looking at cat food? We haven't got a cat! You're a strange creature, Billy Plimpton!" I had to duck down really quickly like I was scratching my ankle. So that Blakemore didn't see me. The last thing I want is for Mum to embarrass me in front of him. He would definitely use that against me. When the coast was clear, I snuck another look at him. They were choosing yoghurt and he had his head down looking at the floor. He looked like a really little kid that day.

Today I sit and watch him for ages. He just sits there with his head in his hands. He's much stiller than usual. He doesn't write a single thing the whole time I'm watching. He always comes bottom in maths. He's rubbing his forehead and his cheeks are pink. I try to imagine him at home eating Shreddies, with his mum shouting at him and his big brother shoving him around. I think maybe Blakemore's not a happy kid. I wonder to myself what would I rather, be like Blakemore without a stammer, or be like me?

While me and Skyla are eating our chips at lunch I have an idea. "D-Do you want to come to the theatre after this?" I say, trying to act relaxed.

"What, to sit in silence and stare at an empty stage?"

"No." I pause and then go for it. "To watch me do some jokes . . . *on* the stage."

She doesn't say anything, she just shoves the last of

her chips in her mouth and grabs her tray, and with a mouth full of food she looks at me and says, "LET'S GO, FUNNY BOY."

It feels really strange actually having someone looking back at me, instead of row after row of empty chairs. I go red and don't know what to do with my hands but after a couple of jokes I start to relax.

Skyla sits right in the middle and laughs at everything but she REALLY laughs when I'm doing impressions of the teachers. I'm just making it up on the spot, after I have finished my set list. Falling asleep and forgetting everyone's names, while talking about the periodic table in a wobbly high-pitched voice, like Mrs Carpenter in chemistry. Pretending to be Mr Randall, the head of maths. Jumping around and clapping my hands together, like an excitable puppy:

"G-G-Go on, class, throw the ball, I'll fetch it. P-P-Please please please please. W-Woof," and then I run off for an imaginary ball and stop in the middle of the stage to scratch an itch on my back that is just out of reach. When I do this Skyla howls with laughter.

She makes me do that impression over and over again until we both have tears rolling down our faces. When the beaky-faced ballet teacher comes in and says, "What on earth is going on in here?" it just makes us laugh even more. Somehow we manage to mumble, "Sorry," grab our bags and fall out of the door into the corridor, tears still streaming.

"I don't think I'm ever going to stop laughing," Skyla says, wiping her eyes.

I look at her and am about to tell her about signing up to the talent show when the beaky teacher stomps back out of the theatre and looks at us like an angry bird. We both look down at the floor, trying to control our shrieks of laughter. I think I'll leave the talent show as a surprise.

At afternoon break Blakemore ties me to the basketball post with a skipping rope from the gym. Then he makes me beg him to be released.

"Say, 'pretty pretty please', Plimpton."

"P-P-P-P-P-P-P-P-P—"

When he gets bored of waiting for me to finish he just walks off and kicks a basketball over the wall, leaving me firmly attached to the post with no way to escape.

Skyla finds me and tries to undo me but she can't untie the knot. He has pulled the rope too tight and it's wet. Skyla's getting really cross and says she'll kill him. Mrs Peat the food tech teacher can't undo the knot either. I have to stay there for ages in the drizzle. Everyone's laughing. A big group of Year Tens gather round me and some of them get their phones out and film me. I try so hard not to cry but I can feel my throat getting tight and a tear comes out of my eye by accident. I can't stop it from rolling down my cheek and I can't wipe it away.

Eventually Matthew, Josh and Alex come running over with some big scissors from the art cupboard and cut me free. Mrs Peat sends William Blakemore to see Mr Osho, and me, Matthew, Alex, Josh and Skyla all have to go too.

Blakemore just says that we'd been "messing about". I don't want to say anything different so I just nod. It'll only get worse if I say anything. I know the boys won't tell, he is horrible to them too, but then I see Skyla start to speak. She sees me looking at her, I shake my head and mouth the word, *Please*, and she stops.

Mr Osho looks really worried and I feel sorry for him. He can't do anything unless we tell him, and he knows from the look on my face that I'm not saying a word.

Mr Osho tells the others to go but keeps me and Blakemore in the room. I feel a bit sick when it's just us. I didn't realize how much better I felt having the others around me until they'd gone. I almost wish I had let Skyla tell Mr Osho everything.

"OK, boys," Mr Osho begins. "Now, I know you are not going to tell me the full story and that's totally up to you but it's clear that something's going on and I wouldn't be doing my job if I didn't try and help you both."

"I don't need any help," Blakemore snarls. He really doesn't even care how he speaks to teachers. I'm amazed he hasn't been kicked out of school yet.

"Everyone needs help with something, William," Mr Osho says, smiling. "You know, in my last school what they used to do if two kids were not getting on was organize a play date at one of their houses."

"W-W-What?!" I say, panicking. Imagining me stuck at Blakemore's house with his mum shouting at me and his massive brother pushing me around.

"Don't worry, we won't do that today, but you know what, it really worked. It made the kids see each other differently and find common ground. So maybe we could do something similar here."

What on earth is he doing? The last thing I need is to spend *more* time with Blakemore. I can't even look at him. If Mr Osho knew about the filming in the toilet, and all of the other horrible things Blakemore has done, maybe he wouldn't be doing this.

"Mr Osho, I n-n-need to t-t-tell you s-s-s-something," I say, and then I look at Blakemore, who cocks his head as if he is interested, and I can't carry on.

Mr Osho waits for a while, and when he realizes that I am not going to say any more, he says, "OK, so I have an idea. William, you've been struggling in maths, right?"

"No."

"Well, that's not what your test results are saying. Billy, maths is your strongest subject, so how about we get together one morning break each week and, Billy, you can be William's very own tutor."

"No way!" me and Blakemore both say at exactly the same time.

"OK, well, in that case, I guess I will have to invite your parents in and see if there is another way of resolving this."

I really don't want Mum coming in, I will never hear the end of it. I can see Blakemore doesn't want his mum to come in either so I say, "Fine, I'll d-d-do it if he w-w-wiill."

"Fine," he spits. "But don't think we are going to be friends."

"Well, let's just see how it goes," says Mr Osho. "How does Wednesday morning sound?"

As we are walking back down the corridor I realize that this is the first time I have even stood next to Blakemore without him doing something awful to me. As we pass the theatre I notice a different poster up next to all of the talent show ones. I stop to look at it and Blakemore keeps going.

"See you Wednesday, B-B-Billy," he says over his shoulder. "I c-c-can't w-w-w-wait!"

Somehow I think it will take more than some maths to make him stop being horrible, but at least Mr Osho will be there to protect me. I look up at the new poster.

WONDERING WHETHER TO ENTER THE TALENT SHOW?

WANT TO JOIN A BAND?
REHEARSE YOUR ACT? HAVE
SOME PRACTICE IN FRONT OF A
SMALL FRIENDLY AUDIENCE?

OPEN REHEARSALS HELD IN THE
MUSIC LOUNGE ON WEDNESDAY
2nd NOVEMBER 12.30-1.30.

COME AND WATCH OR JOIN IN.

"Do you fancy it, Billy? I've seen you eyeing up the drum kit!" Alex is standing behind me.

"Yeah, I really want another go on the kiiit."

I remember Ellie saying that she would be at the rehearsal and it makes me want to go even more. I can't do comedy, not yet – not until I've been on the course – but I could play the drums for her, and I have been practising like crazy since Mr Osho showed me the kit.

"I think you need to be in a band, though," I say

to Alex. "Dooo you play anything?"

Then I realize what I've said is probably a bit stupid, seeing as he can't hear much. I'm about to apologize when he sees the embarrassed look on my face and laughs.

"As crazy as it sounds, my mum has made me learn the piano for the last seven years. I don't know why. I can't even hear what I'm playing! She says 'reading music is a skill everyone should learn'."

"That's pretty awesome," I say.

"I guess so. Mum just treats me the same as my brothers. They have piano lessons, so I have them. It makes no difference that I can't hear as well. I just learn it a bit differently, I guess." Then he becomes his mum again. "It's good to be different, Alex. Use it to your advantage.'"

Alex does a great impression of his mum. He puts on this high voice and swishes his hair. I'm still laughing when the last bell goes and the corridor's instantly filled with kids. I grab the flyer from the board and stuff it into my pocket.

At The Oaks after school I rush in and nearly bump headfirst into Mrs Gibbens, who is slowly making her way out of Granny Bread's room, still clinging on to the picture of the dog. I mumble an apology and try not to look at her too much. She's like a living ghost. When I've edged round her I see Granny Bread in her usual spot in front of *Countdown*.

"I can't even see the letters any more, Billy. I don't know why I still watch the daft thing. Turn it off, sweetie, and tell me about your day."

"Well, I have some big news for you," I say, barely able to keep my excitement in.

"Go on, then, this sounds fun."

"It is! I've entered a talent sh-show, Granny Bread! I'm going to tell my jokes on a stage, just like you wanted me to. Remember the promise I made? Well, this is it, I'm going to do it."

"Well, Billy." She smiles and grabs my face between her tiny hands and looks me right in the eye. "I'll be there in the front row cheering you on. I can't wait!" Then she holds out her little finger and we make our pinky promise all over again.

CHAPTER 17

**What does a cat like to eat on his birthday?
Jelly and mice cream.**

I'm twelve years old! I like being twelve. Next year all the grown-ups will be going on about me being thirteen. They've already started! *Not long now till you're a teenager!* As if it's an original thing to say. Just like when I was ten. I kept count of how many people said, "Double figures!" to me. It was forty-eight, and that's not including the ones who said it first and gave me the idea of counting. So I reckon it was more like sixty. That's a lot of people repeating the same thing. I didn't know what to say. What are you meant to say to that?

Chloe has the same thing now but with her wobbly tooth. "You need to tie a piece of string to that and attach it to the door handle." Over and over again. I can see the look on her face when yet another person says it. Not knowing what they want from her. I'm counting for her too. So far it's seventeen, but could get much higher if the tooth doesn't fall out for ages. I'm betting it gets to over twenty-five. I told her I'm keeping score. She smiled like she was glad that someone had noticed and then carried on dressing her pony.

When there's a knock at the door this morning I run to answer it, hoping it's something for my birthday. A pale-looking delivery man is standing on the doorstep and asks, "Where do you want the drum kit?" I nearly explode!

I read the note:

Dear Billy,
    Don't worry what anyone else says... Make some noise and just enjoy yourself! I might even be able to hear you from here! You are the best grandson in the world and I love you so much.
    Granny Bread.

Mum says under her breath, "I think she's losing her marbles," when she reads it.

I can't believe Granny Bread bought it for me. I

don't think Mum and Dad are too pleased. She didn't even tell them!

I get dressed as fast as I can and run all the way to The Oaks without stopping. I'm totally out of breath and when I get to her little room I hug her so hard. She's chuckling and saying, "my boy," over and over. I can feel her thin body underneath her dressing gown; it feels like it's going to break. Apparently she got one of the care workers at The Oaks to order it online for her. She said she had some savings and wanted to give me something really special. Then she falls asleep while I'm talking to her, so I don't even get to say goodbye properly.

A full-size drum kit! I thought I would be practising with pencils for ever. I love it so much. When I get back Dad's setting it up in the garage, but he doesn't look too happy. I play it for four hours non-stop until I start to get blisters on my hands. Then Mum comes in and says the neighbours have complained so we "need to put some rules in place".

I wish I had a soundproof studio so I could play all day every day. Dad says it's probably a good thing to limit it; otherwise he says I'll lose my hearing! He's making me wear ear defenders, which are these stupid-looking earmuff things. I don't see the point of them. Drums are meant to be loud! I'll only wear them when he's with me.

I'm working on my double-stroke rolls (that's like a normal drum roll but you hit it twice with each stick). It's hard. Dad got his old guitar out of the loft and played it with me. I didn't even know he could play the guitar. He's pretty good! It feels like a proper band. I think we should be called The Sharks.

It feels so good when we get into a rhythm together, like we're talking to each other with music. Like it's a different language. He calls it being in the zone and I think he loves it just as much as me. So I think the drums are here to stay.

Mum and Dad got me this cool microphone for my birthday, so I can practise my jokes. It looks like real gold and has buttons you can push to change your voice. When I'm not allowed on the drums any more, I do a show for them in the living room. I make my voice sound like a chipmunk and go through my latest jokes.

"Why are seagulls called seagulls? B-B-Because if they flew over the bay, they'd be bagels!" Chloe wees her pants she's laughing so much at this one.

After the show in the living room, I put the microphone on the top shelf in my room so I can look at it when I go to sleep. I've decided that I'm not going to use it again until I have been on the course. So that I can speak into it properly. It's exciting, looking at it. Knowing that the next time I use it I'll be able to speak without a stammer.

The stammer school still haven't emailed me back. They'd better hurry up, it starts in a week! I've already started packing and repacking my bag in secret. I've packed my favourite blue hoodie and my black jeans to wear on the box at the end. I'm hiding the bag at the back of my wardrobe.

When I come downstairs I see a big envelope with my name on it lying on the floor under the postbox. The postman's already been, with my cards from great-aunties I've never met and presents from my cousins, so I can't think who this would be from. When I open it I know straight away. It is a handmade book with a beautiful drawing of a stage with velvet curtains and in the spotlight is a picture of me with a microphone. At the top it says:

The Never-Ending Joke Book

by

Billy Plimpton

Illustrated by Skyla Norkins

Inside on each page is one of my favourite jokes with a cartoon drawn alongside it. It must have taken Skyla ages. When I get to the end there are loads of empty pages with the words:

IF YOU NEVER STOP TELLING THEM, I WILL NEVER STOP DRAWING THEM...

I feel a bit overwhelmed, so I slap myself on the cheeks and say, "Pull yourself together, Bill! You are twelve years old, for goodness' sake," and then I take my very own joke book and put it on my shelf with all the others. I can't believe Skyla remembered all my jokes. Maybe that's what she has been doing at lunchtimes, spending all of her time drawing them so beautifully. I can't wait until she sees me up on that stage, telling them properly for the first time.

Matthew, Josh and Alex all arrive in the afternoon and I have my first ever sleepover.

When they get here we have my favourite tea, macaroni cheese with big dollops of pesto and garlic bread. Then we have a Nerf gun war in the woods at the end of the lane. Mum and Dad give us all a Nerf gun and two hundred bullets! Chloe doesn't want to play and so stands at the edge with her pom-poms cheering us on.

The teams are me, Alex and Mum against Dad, Josh and Matthew, with Chloe watching. We have to rescue a Toblerone from a tree and get it back to our base without getting shot. If we do it we can eat it. We have three games and we win two of them. Afterwards we share out the Toblerone and then Mum, Dad and Chloe go back home. Me and the boys stay and play until our fingers go numb from the cold, then when it's too hard to pull the trigger we go in for hot chocolate and birthday cake.

After cake we play on the drums. Matthew has a go on Dad's guitar. He's started lessons at school and he's pretty good. Josh plays the tambourine as that's the only other instrument we have. I do an impression of Josh jiggling around with a tambourine, like he can't stop playing it. Josh joins in and we keep jumping around the garage until we're all laughing so hard. We don't have a piano for Alex so he plays Chloe's old toy xylophone.

When we play we actually sound OK. I ask them if they'll play at the rehearsal day in the Music Lounge so that I can have a go on the drum kit at school. I don't tell them that I want to play for Ellie. No way! They say they'll think about it. After that we watch *Jumanji* in my room and eat popcorn.

Alex falls asleep at 10.30 p.m.! I can't believe it. Especially as he bet me five Quality Street that he would stay up the latest. Alex is really competitive. Once he bet me a pound that he could hold his breath for longer than me. I won by twenty seconds, but he never gave me my pound. Josh and Matthew both fall asleep before midnight. We haven't even had the feast.

I end up eating both bags of M&M's and all the Haribos and then feel really sick and have to go and have a cuddle with Mum at midnight. I get really sweaty and think I'm going to vomit on her. Lucky for her I don't. She takes big breaths with me until it passes. I feel like a little kid again.

Not quite how I had planned it. My sleepover. When I feel a bit better I sneak back in, Mum says I have to, "so that they don't wake up without the birthday boy". I'm top to toe with Alex. It's so dark and he's so still I have to check he's still alive. I touch his toes with my fingers, and when he rolls over I nearly jump out of my skin!

It takes ages to get to sleep after that. Thinking about my birthday and my friends all snoring around me. I actually have friends! All I need now is for the stammer course to email me back. I check again before I go to sleep. I don't know why it's taking so long. As soon as I have got rid of my stupid stammer my life will be complete. Although, to be honest, my birthday felt pretty complete just as it was. Lying in bed, listening to the snores, looking up at my beautiful joke book and my microphone, I actually feel happy. Properly happy.

CHAPTER 18

Why did Cinderella get kicked off the football team?
Because she kept running away from the ball.

After Alex, Matthew and Josh have all packed up their sleeping bags and been picked up, I try to tell Mum that I'm still feeling too sick from all the Haribo to go to football, but she doesn't believe me.

"You do this every week," she says, as she packs Chloe's dance things into a bag. I try to look more ill but she isn't buying it. "I've got to take your sister to dance rehearsal. Do you want to come to that instead?" I shake my head. "Your dad's filming. Come on, Billy, make it easy for me."

I feel like saying, "Make it easy for *me*! You have no idea how hard my life is. So why don't you make it easy for me?!" but then I think about my drum kit in the garage, my microphone, my sleepover and all of my other presents, so I don't say any of that. I definitely don't want to go to a stupid dance rehearsal, so I get my goalie gloves and boots and go and listen to music in the car.

When we get there Mum just lets me out in the car park, shouts through the window, "Bye, sweetie. Good luck!" and pulls away. By the time I've seen him it's too late, she's already driven off. I can see the top of Chloe's head disappear as the car turns out on to the road. I have to stop myself from chasing after it. There's panic rising in my tummy. I feel really sick and it's definitely not the Haribo this time.

With all the excitement of my birthday I totally forgot to check who we were playing. It's Beeston Rovers again – Blakemore's team. I look around, desperate for an idea, somewhere to hide, and then I see her. Standing on the sidelines, her hands in her pockets and her red hair blowing into her face, is Ellie. Bannerdale Ellie who's going to watch me play the drums in a few days' time. I think I must be losing my mind. Why would she be here? I look and look. Again and again. She is still there. She sees me looking and gives me a little smile. I'm not sure if she remembers me or if she's just smiling because I'm staring at her. I kind of smile back, but when my coach shouts at me to warm up I tear my eyes away from her and jog over to the others. I can't see Blakemore anywhere and tell myself that he's not playing.

As I'm jumping up and down in the goal to keep warm I spot him on the other side of the field, grinning at me as he's kicking a ball between his feet. When the whistle goes I realize that he's playing up front and so I can't avoid him. I tell myself it can't be too bad; with everyone watching, what's the worst he can do? I can't stop glancing over at Ellie, who's standing with her dad.

Just then the ball hits me hard in the chest. I lose all of the air in my body, in a split second, and fall to my knees. Then I see the ball just in front of me and jump on top of it. I've saved my first goal of the match! Now I really have to concentrate. I *don't* want to look stupid in front of Ellie. When I look up I realize that Blakemore's the one who struck the ball into my chest. He's clearly not happy that I've saved it.

As the game carries on, I'm letting in as many as I'm saving, but it's not too bad. With every goal Beeston score comes a loud hoot and a cheer from him, "Poor B-B-Billy Plimpton," or, "Bad luck, B-B-B-Billy Plimpton."

He's pretty clever in some ways. He knows how to hide what he's doing just well enough to get away with it. Grown-ups just don't know what to do with him. When I look over at Ellie, she looks bored or sad, I can't tell which one.

It's their corner kick and I'm trying to get into a position where I can see what's happening. Corners are always the worst. At my height I can't see a thing. Blakemore's right on top of me. Moving me around the goal with his shoulders. Making himself really tall and towering above me. When the ball comes into the box, everything goes into slow motion. It flies over Blakemore and is heading my way. I raise my arms up and jump as high as I can. He twists his face around, sees that I'm going to reach it and then shoves me hard.

Then time speeds up again. I go flying towards the back of the net. My head hits the back post and I feel dizzy for a minute as I lie on the ground, like I might faint. I shake my head and blink a few times, and as I'm about to get up he's there, standing over me with a grin on his face.

"Billy, you need to be more careful, mate." Then he

gets down and whispers into my ear, "Maybe instead of you teaching me maths, I should be teaching you how to speak." He kneels down and puts his hand hard on my chest, not letting me up. "Do you want to ask me for some help to get up?" I know he's not going to let me up until I ask him.

Just as I start, "W-W-W-Will. . ." Ellie comes into view. She's stormed on to the pitch and looks furious! She grabs Blakemore by the shirt and pulls him off me. Then she pushes him away, hard. He just turns and walks back up the pitch, singing loudly.

She offers me her hand but I just scramble up as quickly as I can. I can't look at her. Then she says, "I'm sorry for my stupid stepbrother. He is an idiot."

Her stepbrother! She *can't* be related to Blakemore. I'm so confused, I feel really strange. When the referee comes over and asks if I'm OK, I say that I'm dizzy and he tells me to go and sit on one of the benches.

I'm trying to take it all in when Ellie brings me some juice and a biscuit from the clubhouse. She smiles and sits down next to me. "Are you OK?"

"Y-Y-Yes, I'm u-used to iiiit." She just sits and looks at me as I speak, and waits. Just like she did when I met her at cross-country.

"You shouldn't *have* to get used to it," she says sadly.

"Do you l-live with him?" I ask.

"God, no! My dad married his mum. I just go over every other weekend, and that's too often, if you ask me. I wish my dad had never got involved with that stupid family." I don't know what to say then, so we just sit there in silence and watch the game. Then out of nowhere she says, "My dad used to have a stammer when he was a kid."

"Did he?" I can't keep the surprise out of my voice. I've never met anyone in real life with a stammer before. I think I've made myself believe that I'm the only one. I don't know what to say. I have so many questions, but the first one that comes out is, "Was it like mine?" I remember the crying cat lady from the documentary and the man having the stammer fit. I wonder if his was like one of them.

"I don't know, I never heard it." She carries on watching the game.

"Well, I am g-g-going on a course next week that's going to get rid of miiine," I say. I've not told anyone about the course, I've not even heard back from them yet, so I'm not sure why I blurt it out to Ellie.

"Really?" she says.

I just nod. I don't know why, but then I get the tight feeling in my throat and my eyes start to go funny, though I don't think she notices.

"Ever since my dad moved in with them, William and his stupid brother Dillan have been awful." She leans back and rests her head, looking up to the sky, the sun making her hair look like it's been lit up. "They both had this idea that their folks would get back together, even though by the sounds of it their dad is a pretty nasty bloke. When my dad proposed I suppose they realized there was no chance of that happening. Dillan takes it out on William. Treats him pretty badly."

"I saw him once, I think," I say, remembering the older boy's angry face.

"That might be why William's so horrible, not that it's an excuse. That, and the fact he absolutely HATES school."

"Really? I can't imagine B-B-Blakemore hating s-s-s-school. He looks like he loves stomping around, b-bullying everyone."

"Oh no, he hates it. Whenever I'm over at my dad's William's always trying to get out of going to school. They end up dragging him crying into the car some mornings. He finds *everything* difficult – he could barely read at primary. They have done loads of tests to find out why. Not that any of that makes it OK to be a horrible person." Then we sit for a while, both looking up to the sky, and she says,

"Are you coming to the Music Lounge next week for the rehearsal?"

"Yes. Definitely!" The words have left my lips before I can even think about what I'm saying.

"Wow! Well, I'll get to hear you drum after all."

When Coach tells Mum about my "head injury" she feels really bad for making me play, so I get to lie on the sofa and watch movies all afternoon while she reads the newspaper.

"Can I fetch you anything, sweetie?" she says as she goes to the kitchen. It's quite nice being looked after, I think. Maybe I should be injured more often.

"Just some juice, please," I say feebly. "Oh, and some crisps?"

"Coming right up," she says, putting her paper down on the coffee table. A headline down at the bottom of the page catches my eye.

**Electrical Stimulation of Brain
Trialled as Aid to Treating Stutter**

I sit up and grab the newspaper. It's all about sending electrical impulses to the brain through little sticky pads. I quickly rip out the article before Mum comes back; I'll read it properly later. I'll hide it on my pinboard, underneath all my lists. Just as I'm folding it up, I see, at the bottom of the article, it says that they are just "at the pilot stage" and "it will not be ready for the public for at least another five years". Thank the gods of speech I don't have to wait for this to be ready, five years is way too long...

CHAPTER 19

**What do you call friends who love maths?
Algebros.**

When the bell goes for break on Wednesday morning my heart sinks. A whole twenty-five minutes I have to spend with him. When I walk into the room no one is there and I am tempted to turn and run, but as I spin around, there he is.

"How's your head, Billy?" he says, smirking. Behind him is Mr Osho.

"What happened to your head?" asks Mr Osho, as we make our way in.

"Juuust f-f-football at the weekend, sir. We p-played against each other. Nothing to do with school."

"Bad tackle?" he asks, looking pointedly at Blakemore.

"W-W-Well, sir, it was *almost* a textbook goal," I say, putting on my best sports commentator voice and holding an imaginary microphone to my mouth. "Beeston Rovers are pushing up now and they have won a great corner. The pressure is really on for Hartwell. Richards c-c-c-crosses the ball in high to Blakemore. Blakemore seems blinded by the lights of the stadium. W-W-What's happening? B-B-Blakemore has mistaken Plimpton's head for the ball! These are d-devastating scenes of football. Plimpton's head f-f-flies in off the post and straight into the back of the net. Textbook."

Blakemore can't help but laugh at this.

"Sounds painful, Billy," says Mr Osho. "It's clearly not knocked any of the funny out of you, though, has it?"

I feel a bit different with Blakemore when Mr Osho is here, like I can be more myself, without being so terrified.

"OK, boys, it seems like this is more important than ever. I'm going to do some marking and you can work on this week's homework. Sound good?"

"Fine," we both say at the same time, although the way Blakemore says it is very different to the way I do.

I've already finished my homework so I just wait for Blakemore to get his out.

"What you looking at?" he mumbles and I see Mr Osho looking up from his desk.

"I've already done mine so I'll just help you," I whisper. Mr Osho goes back to his marking.

As he gets his maths homework out I see his other books in his bag, all frayed and bent. His maths book is covered in doodles of skulls and crossbones.

"Nice skulls," I whisper.

I can tell he wants to say something mean but he looks at Mr Osho and stops himself.

The homework is all algebra. As he is looking for the right page in his book I can see that he has not done any of the previous homework sheets. They are all just scribbled over or blank. I look at him and can see his cheeks going red as he flips through the pages. He has the look on his face from the exam. Like a little boy. I can see that he really doesn't want to make a start and so I say, in a half-whisper,

"H-How about I show you how I would work the first one out and then you can do the second?"

"How about you just do it for me?" he whispers.

"How about," comes Mr Osho's voice, cutting across our whispers, "I check your work at the end? So I know that you understand what you have written?"

I give Blakemore an apologetic look, and shrug my shoulders. I take out my pens and hand him one.

By the time the bell goes we have not managed a single question. I kept explaining it over and over and showing him the working out until he nodded but then when it was his turn he still couldn't do it. It was like he just couldn't see it, like his brain was getting stuck.

"This is so pointless," he says.

"It's a bit like me with speaking. The harder you try, the worse it gets?"

"Yeah, I suppose," he says, closing his book.

"How was that, boys?" Mr Osho says, gesturing to have a look at the book in Blakemore's hand.

"There's nothing to show you," mumbles Blakemore.

"Pardon, William?"

"There's nothing to show you, OK?" Blakemore shouts. "I can't do it. I won't ever be able to do it. There's no point me even being here, it's embarrassing." Even though he sounds angry he looks like he's going to cry, I can see tears forming in his eyes. I can't believe it, William Blakemore *crying*.

"OK, not to worry. These things take time. You're not going to give up on him, are you, Billy?"

"N-No, sir," I say, and in that moment I actually mean it. I want to help William Blakemore. As I am leaving, Mr Osho says, "Billy, can you stay back a minute?" and we watch Blakemore skulk off, with his shoulders low.

"I hope you are not too cross with me for asking you to do this?" he says, biting his thumbnail.

"No, sir."

"Even though you won't admit it, I know what's going on, Billy, OK?"

I just nod.

"There's only so much I can do if you don't talk about it, but I just want you to know that I've got your back. I won't let this carry on, OK?"

"I just wish everything was a bit easier, sir."

"Me too, Billy. Sometimes there's only one thing for it," and with that he hands me a pair of drumsticks, takes out his trumpet from his desk and says, "Shall we?"

At lunch I look around for Skyla. She's been off school all week and I have not seen her properly since I got my joke book. This morning I asked Mr Osho if she was OK, and he said she was due to come back in at lunch. I can't see her anywhere, though, and so start eating my chips. I really want to do another show for her in the theatre. To run through my talent show set again. As I'm leaving the lunch hall she appears at the doors, looking scruffier than usual. Her hair is all over the place.

"Are y-y-y-you OK?" I ask.

"Yeah, I'm fine," she says.

"Where've you been?"

"Mum's been really bad the last couple of weeks so I stayed at home to keep an eye on her."

"That s-sounds rough," I say.

"Yeah, well, I'm back now, to the wonders of Bannerdale High! What's new?"

"I've n-n-not seen you since my birthday," I say. "Your present is THE BEST thing I've ever seen."

"Easy, tiger. I don't think so. I just didn't have any money so thought I would make you something instead. It's a bit lame."

"No, I love it."

I almost want to hug her. She looks so sad and alone and I don't think she understands how much I love her present, but as I'm looking at her I see Ellie walking down the hall and stop myself.

"H-Hi, Ellie!" I say, trying to sound casual. She

doesn't hear me, and with that Skyla turns down the corridor.

"See you in class, Bilbo," she calls.

When I get home I look through all my old maths books to try and remember how I learned algebra. When Chloe gallops by on an imaginary pony she gives me an idea.

"Chloe, d-do you know what algebra is?"

"A disease?"

"Ha! No, it's to do with maths. Do you w-want me to show you?"

"I hate maths."

"I can make it about ponies."

She still looks unsure.

"And I will give you one of my b-b-birthday chocolates."

"OK!" and she gallops over and ties up her make-believe horse to the dishwasher.

Five of my birthday chocolates and a lot of unicorns and ponies in various imaginary pens later, I think Chloe has got the vague idea. Obviously Blakemore would stove my head in if I suggested using horses and mythical creatures to do his homework, but I feel like I can give it a go. I just need to find out what he likes.

CHAPTER 20

Doctor: I have some bad news and some very bad news.

Patient: Well, you might as well give me the bad news first.

Doctor: The lab called with your test results. They said you have twenty-four hours to live.

Patient: Twenty-four hours! That's terrible! What's the very bad news?

Doctor: I've been trying to reach you since yesterday.

My stammer has been *so* bad this week. It's weird. Everything at school was getting better, my friends are awesome and my jokes are definitely getting funnier. The other afternoon on my daily visit to

The Oaks, Granny Bread said that she thought she couldn't breathe, she was laughing so hard. I was doing impressions of Mum and Dad telling me off. I've got Mum perfectly now: "Billy Plimpton, get in here this minute. What on earth are five pairs of your shoes doing on my kitchen floor? It's not a shoe shop. Treat this house with more respect, please, or I will lose it." I sound exactly like her, the voice and the way she breathes in at the end of a sentence.

I had to call one of the nurses in when Granny Bread would not stop wheezing, who told me that maybe I should "lay off the jokes for a bit".

Granny Bread said, "NEVER!" really loudly and then burst out laughing again.

I even think that William Blakemore might not be as mean to me when I've found a way to help him with maths. So you would think my stammer would get better, not worse. That's not always how it works, though. Sometimes it makes sense and gets worse when I'm tired or stressed and things are all rubbish, but sometimes everything seems fine and it just gets in the way for no reason. It's so annoying.

In drama with Mrs Gallagher today we are all sitting in a circle and she asks us to say a joke, a riddle or a fact. *Brilliant!* I think as I mentally start sifting through all of my jokes from my latest top ten list.

I am near the end of the circle and as everyone's taking their turns I'm getting more excited and impatient. I've thought of the perfect one that I have not tried out on anyone yet. I read it in a joke book in the library. I'm just editing it in my head to make it sound more realistic.

Today over breakfast, ~~my husband~~ my dad asked, "Have you got a bookmark?" and I burst into tears. I'm ~~42~~ 12 years old and he still doesn't know my name is ~~Sarah~~ Billy.

I'm going over and over it in my head trying to get the wording just right, deciding what voice to do for the crying bit. Yasmin starts telling a riddle about a horse and gets muddled up and tells people the answer by accident. Everyone starts giggling and she starts looking really embarrassed. All of a sudden a massive sense of dread pops into my head. *I can't do this. Everyone will laugh at me.* At that same moment Mrs Gallagher says, "Billy?"

I try to ignore the doubt and rush into the joke.

"T-T-T-T-T-T-T-T-T-T-T-T-T—" I take a big breath in and try again. "T-T-T-T-T-T-T-T-T—" I try a soft "T" like Big Softie says, "Oday," but then I get just as stuck on the "M". I can see everyone's awkward faces, a couple of people trying not to giggle. Mrs Gallagher waits for ages but I don't make it past the word "book" before I give up and sit down, my head on my knees. I just want to run away and hide.

I feel bad for the rest of the day and try not to speak to anyone. I sit in silence at lunch with Skyla.

"You OK, Bilbo?" she says.

I just nod and pack away my tray without saying a word. Then I walk around the corridors on my own instead of going to the Music Lounge. I can't wait until this stammer has gone. I HATE it.

When I get home the first thing I do is check my emails and there's one waiting for me from the stammer school!

Dear Billy,

Thanks for getting in touch.

I'm afraid our courses are not suitable for someone as young as twelve years of age. Our courses were developed to help adults who stammer. Our approach would be too intensive and too physically, psychologically and emotionally demanding for a twelve-year-old. We have had some success with

teenagers, so feel free to get back in touch
in a year or two.

I'm sorry I am unable to help further at
this stage. Maybe the British Stammering
Association could suggest a suitable therapy
option in your area? Their website is www.
stammering.org.

Best wishes,

Brian

When I read the email in my bedroom I get really
hot and cross. I slam the iPad down and scream at
myself in the mirror. My face goes red and I look
really scary. Scared and scary. Thoughts running
through my head. Too many thoughts. They feel loud
and as if they're coming from somewhere else, not
from me. I see the list on the pinboard with only one
option on it.

1. Go on the stammer course

It's like it's laughing at me. Saying it over and over. *Go
on the stammer course, go on the stammer course, go
on the stammer course*. I grab it and screw it up into
a tight ball in my fist, so hard that I see my knuckles

turning white and red. The thoughts filling my brain. Louder and louder. I put my hands over my ears but I can still hear the thoughts.

So that's it, then. You will be stuck like this for ever. Not even able to tell a joke in a stupid drama class, let alone onstage.

I slump down on to the bed. What if it's just going to get worse and worse? I can't wait for "a year or two". I have to fix it now. The thoughts keep coming.

You can't make your mum and dad proud of you now.

You are not *funny, you never will be.*

You told Ellie that you were getting rid of your stammer next week. She'll think you're a liar.

You will be bullied by Blakemore for ever and there is nothing you can do about it. You are pathetic.

The thoughts keep flooding my brain one after another.

What about the talent show? You have promised *Granny Bread. She will be* so *disappointed.*

I imagine telling Granny Bread and the look on her face. I can't cope with the image and start rubbing my head hard like I'm trying to get it out.

I start crying at my reflection and when I can't look at myself any more, I grab my joke books from my bookshelf and throw them all in the bin, Skyla's beautiful drawing facing up at me. Then I throw myself on to my bed and put a pillow over my head.

"STUPID STAMMER. S-SSTUPID STAMMER. STUPID STAMMER," I shout into the pillowcase.

I'm hitting the pillow hard, trying to beat the stammer out of my brain. Surely there is a way to get rid of it. I need it out. Out of my brain. NOW.

That's when I remember the newspaper article. I find it hidden among my lists. Maybe I can do this. Get rid of it on my own. All I need is to get a current into my brain to reprogram it. Shock it into being normal.

I jump out of bed and grab my alarm clock and rip the batteries out of the back. I need to put them in my head. I need to DO something. I feel frantic now, wild and completely out of control. I put one battery on one side of my forehead and the other one on the other side and press as hard as I can. "Work! I n-n-need you to work!" I wait.

Nothing.

Then I remember my circuit science kit and grab it from the shelf. Using sellotape I stick the ends of the wires to my temples and attach the crocodile clips to the batteries. I feel like a mad scientist creating a new invention. I shout to the ceiling, "Please, Gods, m-m-m-make it work!" and flick the little switch. I feel nothing, but maybe the current is still going in.

I remember the people on the DVD putting straps around themselves and so I find a belt and wrap it around my chest and pull it tight. I flick the switch on and off, stare into the mirror and scream, "Work! Do something!"

Mum must have heard the screaming. She comes running in and grabs hold of the batteries, pulls the wires off my head and throws them across the room and holds me tightly. "What are you doing to yourself, my beautiful boy?" She keeps repeating it again and again as she gently undoes the belt. "What are you doing to yourself, my beautiful boy?" She is crying now and so am I. Eventually I show her the crumpled piece of newspaper.

So that's it. It's over. I can't do it. My dream of being a comedian and doing the talent show are over. No more jokes. No more theatre.

I can't even think about Granny Bread now, without wanting to scream and cry. I have broken my pinky promise. What happens when you break a promise? Maybe I am about to find out. A shiver runs down my spine at the thought.

CHAPTER 21

**I told my friend that onions are the only food
that can make you cry.
He threw a coconut at me.**

Skyla's off school again today so I don't have to
pretend everything's OK to her. She always knows
when I'm lying. Once at lunch when we were telling
each other weird facts about ourselves, I tried to
make her believe that I could hula-hoop for an hour,
but she totally knew I was making it up. I don't
know how she does it. What gives me away. When I
told the same thing to Josh to see if I could work on
my lying face he just said, "Awesome!" and carried
on jiggling. Then I felt bad for lying so I said, "I'm
only joking, I can't really." He stopped jiggling for a
minute and said, "Billy, sometimes your jokes make

no sense," and then rubbed his hands together.

I must look terrible this morning as Alex knows that something's wrong as soon as I walk into class. I just say that I'm not feeling well, but he looks at me right in the eyes with this funny expression on his face. He has his eyes crossed and his tongue lolling out. He doesn't stop until I smile. It's nice having Alex around.

Before lunch I run straight down to the office to cross my name off the talent show list. I haven't told Mum anything about that. She would only try and make me do it anyway. She doesn't understand. No one does.

Just as I'm scribbling over my name I feel someone standing behind me.

"What ya' doing, Billy Plimpton?" It's Blakemore. My stomach flips over a thousand times as I turn to face him. I look at the office desk and the lady with the mole isn't there. "You entering the talent show?" he sneers. "What a brilliant idea!" He looks really pleased with himself.

"N-N-N-N-N-NO," I say, shaking my head fast. I'm ahead of him. I know this isn't good.

"You ARE entering the talent show, aren't you, Billy? Oh, look, there seems to be a mistake. Your name's crossed out. Let me fix that for you."

Then he grabs my hand and forces me to write my name on the list. As my hand is being moved around the paper and I see my name appear, I want to scream. I don't have the strength to fight him and so I just let him. A tear silently rolls down my cheek.

"I wanna see you on that stage, Billy Plimpton. If I don't see you on that stage, I'll be really upset. You think you saw me upset on Wednesday, don't you, Plimpton, but you were wrong."

"I've f-f-figured out a waaay t-to help y-y-you," I say, "w-w-with algebra." Even as I'm saying it I know that I sound ridiculous, desperate. Blakemore howls with laughter.

"I'm a lost cause, Plimpton, and you know it."

"Well, I m-m-may as well try. W-W-We h-h-have to do it anyway."

"OK, fine. If you teach me how to do algebra, before the talent show, you can cross your name off this list."

"Fine!" I say.

"See you Wednesday, Plimpton."

Just then the office lady comes back and smiles. "Brave boy!" she says as Blakemore bounces away down the corridor.

I take a big breath in and look down at my name on the list. I'm shaking. I can't do my stand-up routine at the talent show. Not now. Not now that my plan to get rid of my stammer has well and truly failed. I need a new plan. Maybe like in the show-and-tell I can think of a way to do it without speaking.

In the Music Lounge, Mr Osho brings in his box bass from home and lets everyone have a go. Mum called the school and told him that I tried to "electrocute" myself. That's the word she keeps using, but I told her that's not what I was doing. She makes it sound way worse than it is. Mr Osho keeps asking if I'm OK and watching me.

The box bass is really cool. It's like a big wooden box that you sit on and it has one long string attached to a handle made from a broom. It sounds a bit like a proper big double bass. He made it himself out of an old whisky crate. Everyone has a go at finding a rhythm and playing along to Aretha Franklin. Moving the broom handle to make different notes on the string. Matthew looks funny sitting on the box, his knees up near his chin. It looks like he might break it. Alex is pretty good, but Josh is the best. He's amazing. He jiggles his knees along to the music the whole time and somehow knows how to play.

Mr Osho dances like he's totally forgotten we're here, his head down, nodding from side to side, and his hands in little fists in front of him. I sit on my own on one of the beanbags, too busy thinking about Blakemore and the talent show to join in. But then ... when I look up and see them all laughing and dancing, Josh keeping the rhythm, I start to feel an idea forming in my brain. When the song ends and Mr Osho stops dancing he says that we are "true jazz heads" and that he'll bring in his trumpet one day for a proper jam.

I have to bribe Matthew with a Mars Bar, but the others seem up for it without chocolate-based encouragement, especially Josh, he's really excited. We are going to do the open rehearsal as a jazz band ... and then I'm going to convince them to do the talent show! That way if I can't teach Blakemore anything, which based on last Wednesday seems likely, it won't matter. I can do the talent show anyway.

I'm going to be a drummer instead of a stupid comedian! Apparently "drummers are always in demand", that's what Mr Osho says. As a drummer I don't have to speak. Blakemore didn't say *what* I had to do onstage, just that he wanted to see me there. Granny Bread will still see me on the stage too. It all makes sense.

As soon as they all say yes, I feel a little bit better. Excited, even. We're going to practise at my house after school. We ask Mr Osho what song we should play for the open rehearsal.

"You entering as a band?" he says. "Surely you need to be up there telling your jokes, Billy?"

"N-No, I have given up on the j-j-jokes," I say.

"Really? That makes me very sad," he says.

"I w-w-want to b-be a d-drummer now," I say, trying to sound confident.

"Maybe just leave the door open, Billy. Never give up on something you love." He pats me on the back. "You're one funny boy, don't forget that."

"I j-j-j-just want to f-focus on music for a while," I whisper, looking down at the floor, trying to sound casual.

"Well, that I can definitely help with." He gives me a wink and then writes a list of songs for us to listen to, but says, "Just go with the flow, the rehearsal is just a practice run to see how you all sound together." He even says he'll come along and play the trumpet with us! When I get home I go to my room and listen to everything on the list.

1. "Take the A Train"
2. "Caravan"
3. Anything by Fela Kuti
4. "There Will Never Be Another You"
5. Anything by Miles Davis

As I listen I know there's no chance of us playing anything like this!

Just as I'm googling "Take the A Train", I notice my joke books are back on the shelf, next to my microphone, Skyla's beautiful drawings looking out at me from the shelf. Mum has obviously found them in the bin. I don't want to look at them. They just remind me of everything. I don't want to tell jokes. It's not who I am any more.

I feel a bit sick, so I grab the books and the microphone, wrap them up in some toilet roll and put them all in the bathroom bin. I need to forget all that now and focus on the band.

CHAPTER 22

What do you get when you cross a dog and a calculator?
A friend you can count on.

Another stupid speech appointment. I'm really annoyed because we're making apple crumble in food tech and I'm missing it. It feels pointless going to speech therapy now, but Mum says I have to. "We need to give the DVD back anyway!" she says. I should have put the stupid DVD in the bin with the microphone and the joke books.

I'm meant to be in a pair with Josh for food tech. We've written out the recipe and everything. I told him I was going to the doctor and so wouldn't be in today. When he asked why, I made up a lie about having headaches, but I could feel my face going red as I said it. I don't want *anyone* at Bannerdale to know that I have speech therapy, it's embarrassing. All anyone would think is, *Well, it's clearly not working, is it?*

I don't talk the whole way to Sue's. When we pull into the car park, Mum asks, "Are you OK, honey?"

"I am fine! W-W-Why do you a-a-always ask me thaat?"

"It's just you used to love our mornings coming to see Sue."

"I juuust want to be at school, th-that's all."

"Well, that's great, hon. That's all I needed to know. You have to tell me things or I have no idea what's going on for you." She looks really sad and lost. I feel bad, so I say sorry and we get out of the car.

Sue's waiting for us in the little office with the two-way mirror. She looks a bit different. Her hair is down and she has light pink lipstick on. I know she's going to say something important when we sit down. I can just tell.

"So I want to start this session by telling you my news." She seems a bit nervous. I wonder what on earth she's going to tell us. I immediately start listing the possibilities in my head.

1. She's found out that I emailed the stammer school and is really cross with me?
2. She's called the police about me trying to "electrocute" myself?
3. Mr Osho's called her to say I'm not trying hard enough to talk in class?
4. She knows about the microphone and books in the bin?
5. My stammer is just going to get worse and worse until I can't say anything ever again?

She puts her hands together on her knee and continues. "I've handed in my notice and am moving to Cornwall. So, Billy, this will be my last session with you." She smiles a kind of frowny smile and breathes out of her nose loudly. I don't know what the appropriate way to respond is, so I don't say anything. "I have really enjoyed seeing you grow up and it has been a real pleasure getting to know you over the years, Billy. I know you're having a tough time and so now isn't the best timing. I'm sorry for that. You are a remarkable young man, Billy."

Again, I'm unsure what I'm meant to do. Should I be smiling or not? Does she want me to cry? I like Sue. She's very friendly and kind but I don't feel like

I need to cry. She looks like she might cry, though. I realize that I definitely need to say something now, as the room has been quiet for too long.

"Why are you g-g-going to Cornwall?" I ask.

She laughs. "We've always wanted to live by the sea and when I saw a job come up we realized that if we did not do it now we might never do it. If there's one thing that this work has taught me, it's that you need to be kind to yourself and follow your dreams."

That's two things, I think to myself. "Wiiill I have to see s-s-s-s-s-someone else, then?" I ask.

"Well, that's what we need to talk about today."

Then she looks normal again and tells me all about another lady called Jo who will be taking on her clients. I stop listening as she's talking about a book Jo's written and I start to picture what's on the other side of the magic mirror. I imagine myself telling jokes into my microphone, but like the sound is turned right down. Talking through a mirror and no one being able to hear it. My jokes ending to total silence. Then I realize that there's another silence that I am clearly supposed to fill.

"I don't think I want to have speech therapy any more," I say.

On the way back to school Mum says that I can

change my mind if I want to. She says it four times. On the fourth time I think I'm going to keep count. I bet it will be up to fifteen times by Christmas. I won't change my mind. However many times she asks me. I don't want to go back. I don't want to meet Jo. There's no point any more, if I'm not going to be a comedian after all. I can just be a drummer with a stammer. I'm glad Sue's going to Cornwall. She must have got bored in that room, looking at that mirror all day long. Wondering if anyone was behind it. I hope she swims in the sea every day and sees an octopus.

When I get to school Josh finds me at break. He's saved me some of his apple crumble. I take it round to The Oaks after school, Mrs Gibbens is there again, which is a bit annoying. She is always there now – I want it to be just me and Granny Bread, but Granny Bread doesn't seem to mind her hanging around all the time. When I show them the apple crumble they both want to try some and so I feed it to Granny Bread from a plastic spoon. I think she really likes it. I definitely don't want to feed Mrs Gibbens, but luckily when I hold out the other empty spoon she reaches out and takes it and helps herself. It's a bit like looking after two strange tiny wrinkly old babies, I think to myself, and then feel instantly bad.

When Mrs Gibbens has gone, Granny Bread whispers,

"She was crying earlier, poor woman."

"Why?" I ask, not really wanting to know the answer. Mrs Gibbens still scares me every time I look at her haunted face.

"Before she came here she used to live in a little flat. No family at all. All alone, apart from her little Scraggles. He was her world."

"Is Scraggles the dog in the picture she always carries about?" I ask, slightly interested now.

"She has shown me photo after photo of that scruffy animal. Honestly, Billy, I think that dog was the love of her life."

"Did he die?"

"No," she whispers, and then leans in towards me and looks around as though what she's about to tell me is highly confidential. "That's the tragedy. Here, have some juice and I'll tell you all about it." As I sit back with my strong Ribena, Granny Bread begins the story.

"So, Mrs Gibbens is making herself some soup, in her flat, one Sunday afternoon. Scraggles is curled up in his bed as usual and BOOM, out of nowhere she has this terrible heart attack. She ends up in hospital and she's there for weeks and weeks, poor woman. None of the doctors think she'll make it, she's in a terrible state. When she comes round and realizes where she is, do you know the very first thing she asks about?"

"Scraggles?" I say.

"You've got it."

"Well, what happened to him?" I'm hooked now. Granny Bread really knows how to tell a story.

She pauses and leans in again. "GONE!" she whispers.

"What do you mean, GONE? Where is he?"

"No one knows, Billy. He wasn't there when the ambulance turned up. Not that it would have made any difference. We aren't allowed pets in this place anyway. Not that that makes her feel any better. I don't think a day goes by that she doesn't cry over that ball of fluff. She spends every minute, when she's not in here, staring out of her window hoping to see him. That's never going to happen, poor thing. That's why I invite her round so much. Take her mind off it a bit."

"Surely someone could find him. Put p-posters up or something."

"She brings round pictures to everyone in here and asks us to look out for him. That's no use, though, is it? We are all half-blind or doolally in here! As I said, Billy, she's got no one. No one that would bother. Sad, isn't it? Makes me count my blessings that I've got you; come here and give me a hug."

As we are polishing off what's left of the crumble I tell her that I'm not going to tell jokes at the talent show any more and she looks *really* sad. Even though I tell her I'm going to play the drums instead. I try to sound excited, like it's an even better plan, but she doesn't buy it. She knows me too well. She knows how much I wanted to be a comedian. I think she wanted it just as much.

I feel bad, like I have really let her down. But I just have to concentrate on the band now. We have to get through the open rehearsal and then we can start figuring out what to do for the talent show. I can't embarrass myself in front of Ellie and everyone else. So I can't think about Granny Bread's sad face now.

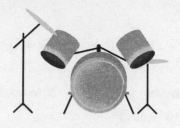

CHAPTER 23

Why was the maths book sad?
It had too many problems.

"W-W-What are you into?" I ask Blakemore as he's getting his maths book out.

"What are you on about?" he scowls.

"What stuff do you like? Then w-w-we can use it in the questions to make them s-s-s-seem more interesting."

"You'll never make maths interesting, Plimpton."

"Just tell m-m-m-me, or else I will use unicorns."

"Fine. *Minecraft*," he says.

"Anything else?"

"No."

"OK, th-th-this could be tricky as I have never

played on M-Minecraft, but that's fine. You can tell me about it."

"You've never played on Minecraft? You are weirder than I thought."

"Is there anything wrong with being different, William?" says Mr Osho, not even looking up from his book.

"No, sir," says Blakemore reluctantly.

When Blakemore starts telling me about the game I get lost pretty quickly, but he seems really excited by it. It sounds to me like it's just like Lego with some characters in it, so that's what I will use. Bricks and baddies.

"I can't draw to save my life," I say, "but you can so I need you to draw a Minecraft wall of bricks, OK?"

When I tell him that there is a special "mystery brick" called X that could be worth more than a single brick he tells me that I sound like his mum, but he's still listening. When I tell him that there is only one way to find out what the mystery brick is worth he rolls his eyes and says,

"A sum?"

"Yes."

He's fine at the easy ones at first and then as soon as I add Y he starts going pink again. I can tell that he's stopped listening and is just trying to get out of it. The more stressed he gets the less he can do it. Then the bell goes and Mr Osho saves us.

"Great work today, boys. See you next week."

"Looks like you are still doing the talent show, Plimpton," says Blakemore as he puts his bag on.

I just smile to myself knowing that I'm going to do it no matter what. He has no idea! He kind of waves at me as he leaves the room so I say, "S-S-Smell you later," and I hear him laugh on the way out.

As I walk past Mr Osho he says quietly, "You're an amazing kid, Billy Plimpton."

The Music Lounge is all set up for the rehearsal day. There are so many instruments. Ellie's on a beanbag with two of her friends. She waves when she sees me and I really want to go and talk to them, but for some reason I feel properly shy and my ears get hot, so I just wave back. Skyla pulls a funny face when she sees me waving at Ellie. When I told Skyla about the band and the talent show, she knew something wasn't right.

"You're playing the drums?" she said, looking at me and waiting for me to go on, when I didn't she said, "OK, I'll come and watch the auditions," but she didn't sound convinced.

I avoid looking at her; I don't want to be reminded of her watching me on the stage, stammering my jokes. It's embarrassing.

It's so busy in the Music Lounge it feels different to normal. You can have a go on any instrument you want. Josh has a go on the huge double bass and I try an electric drum kit. They have even put a table out with biscuits on it and Mr Osho's giving out juice. I have a bit of a headache. I've had a headache since I told Granny Bread that I wasn't doing comedy any more. I'm trying to ignore it.

Then they invite people up to perform. There is a set of twins, one of whom plays the violin and the other does backward walkovers. I'm not sure how the violin really goes together with gymnastics. I don't really like violins, they make my muscles go tense, and it doesn't help my headache at all. Then there's this amazing girl on the piano. Her fingers move so fast and she closes her eyes when she's playing. Then there is a juggler, and then it's us. We're the first band. We've practised twice but we spent most of our time messing about so I'm not exactly sure what we're doing. All we know is that when I get a beat going, Alex can watch me for the rhythm and start a melody on the keyboard. Then the others can join in with his melody.

Mr Osho comes up to the front with us. He's really excited. He introduces us to the kids all sitting around on beanbags and playing board games, which seems a bit much to me. "Ladies and gentlemen, boys and girls, and everyone else. As you may know, I run the lunchtime Music Lounge and the boys here join me in the appreciation of jazz."

He gestures for me to start playing, so I start a low jazz beat, on the ride cymbal – *Ting Ting, T-Ting Ting, T-Ting Ting, T-Ting Ting* – as he continues: "Please put your hands together for The Regulars!" There's a smattering of applause. "On keyboards, we have Alex!" It all seems a bit over the top, considering we can't even play anything, but Mr Osho looks really excited. "...And on the guitar, we have Matthew!" I start to wonder what on earth we're going to play. "And on the box bass, we have Josh!" Josh is jiggling as usual and has a big smile on his face. "And finally, on drums, we have Billy Plimpton." With that Mr Osho gestures for me to up the volume and so I do.

Brr-Rum Pap, Brr-Rum Pap, T-Ting Ting, Brr-Rap-Pap!

It feels good. People listening. Not knowing what's going to happen. No plan at all. Alex comes in with a little loop on the keyboard. It's just me and him for a while. Then I hear Josh's box bass kick in with two big low notes. In a few minutes we're all playing and Mr Osho is at the front, on his trumpet. He's amazing. He takes a solo with just the drums and keyboard underneath and then the others join back in. We're doing it! We're really doing it! I can hear each of them and what they need. The conversation between us all. Without any words at all. I forget about the audience.

We must play for five minutes and at the end we're all out of breath and laughing hard. We hug each other and bow. I look at Ellie and her friends, they're clapping. Mr Osho shouts, "Give it up for The Regulars!" Now that's a good name for a band, I think.

After us there is a magician, who gets all of his tricks wrong, and then a dance group, who constantly forget the steps and start arguing with each other, and then at the end is the last band. Teenplay, they're called. It's the same band I'd seen when they were setting up the room, when I was with Ellie. They are ten times better than us. They have a lead guitarist, whose hair covers his eyes. I wonder how he can see the strings. He does all the singing. There's a bass guitarist with short dark hair and a drummer with very pink cheeks. They look like Year Twelves but

I can't be sure. They play a really loud rock song. They're pretty amazing. Ellie claps loads and whistles with her fingers when they finish. I want her to clap and whistle like that for me.

At the end, when no one else wants to get up, Mr Osho makes a little speech about how great everyone is and then says, "Obviously, today's for everyone, whatever their skill. If any of you have enjoyed performing here, and want to take it up a notch, there is the annual *Bannerdale's Got Talent Show* in December." I look at The Regulars. They all nod at me and put their thumbs up. "For the musicians among us, there is a sign-up sheet for rehearsal slots so you can get in as much practice as you need before the big show!"

As I look at the boys, I think, *Maybe this will be better. I can still do the show and be on the stage. The audience will still be cheering. It is nearly as good as the original dream, just without the jokes, but I'll have my friends by my side.* I can't help feeling a little bit sad, though.

Mr Osho goes on. "We've seen some wonderful musical acts in the past years, along with all sorts of other performers. Dancers, magicians, *comedians*." He looks right at me and winks. "You name it, we have seen it here." My tummy does a flip when he says the word "comedian". I try to shove it down and pretend I have not felt it and avoid his eyes. He carries on: "It was even filmed by our local news team last year! So you could find yourself on the television. But most importantly, enjoy being creative!"

The next day in form class Mr Osho says seeing us play for the first time was one of the best moments of his teaching career. He looks really emotional. He makes us take a vow to start a band called The Regulars and says, "Will you let me come and be a guest trumpeter every now and then? Most importantly, boys, do not forget your jazz roots." So that's the new plan.

Our first proper rehearsal as The Regulars is so much fun. We meet at my house and Dad's put loads of fairy lights and posters of bands up in the garage, or "the studio" as he now calls it. It looks pretty good. We don't play much music as we are laughing too hard; I'm doing my Mr Randall impression and the boys can barely breathe. Mum comes in to bring us some snacks and finds us all on the floor in stitches. We're howling with laughter, unable to stop.

I speak through my tears. "We are going to start soon, I p-promise."

"Don't be daft!" she says. "It's all part of being a band. Just enjoy yourselves." Then she gets that look on her face like she's going to cry.

She's been so worried about me. She won't even let me close the door to my bedroom any more, since the batteries. She even meets me to walk back from Granny Bread's every day. I don't know what she thinks I'm going to do. It's horrible having someone watching you, worrying, all the time. As she looks at me lying there laughing, I think she's just happy that I'm happy. I see her wipe her eyes but I'm laughing too hard to be embarrassed. I think being in The Regulars is going to be a lot of fun.

Maybe this is how it's meant to be. Maybe I was on the wrong path all along. I never needed to get rid of my stammer anyway. I just needed to realize that comedy isn't right for me. That I'm a drummer instead. The talent show might be even more amazing than I had ever dreamed, now that I'm not worrying about my stammer any more.

CHAPTER 24

**What's the difference between a fish and a
piano?**
You can't tuna fish.

Mr Osho has put us down to rehearse every Monday
and Wednesday lunchtime. I feel a bit giddy when
I realize that I might get to see Ellie. I imagine her
sitting on a beanbag while we rehearse, whistling
with her fingers.

After shovelling down my pizza super fast I say,
"Bye," to Skyla and head to the Music Lounge. We
don't know what song we're even going to practise yet,
but it feels exciting. We get there five minutes early
and Teenplay are just at the end of their rehearsal.

We stand in the doorway, watching. When they
get to the end of the song, the boy on the guitar

with the floppy hair says to us, "You were the lads who played the other night with Mr Osho?" We all nod and then he looks at me. "Your drumming was awesome, little man." I laugh and shake my head. As he strums his guitar he says, "Just one more song, boys, then it's all yours."

They start up the same song that I heard them play when I was with Ellie after cross-country. When they get to the tricky section, the drummer stops. They try it a few more times until he throws his sticks down. He looks really cross and his cheeks go brighter pink. "I just can't get it! I'm better on keyboards."

The guitarist looks over to us with a sorry expression on his face. "We're not putting on a very good show for you, are we, lads? Let's pack up and call it a day."

"Seriously, Sam, I just want to go back on keys," the drummer says as he's putting his rucksack on.

Then the floppy-haired boy looks right at me and says, "I don't suppose you want to be the drummer in *our* band, do you, little man?" I can't tell if he's joking but he just keeps looking at me, waiting for an answer.

I laugh and glance at Alex, who just looks down at the floor. Josh is twiddling his tie and Matthew shrugs. I don't know what to do. I feel really trapped.

"It would mean rehearsing every day, though," he adds as he picks up his guitar case.

Just as I'm about to say, "Sorry, I can't," something stops me. I can't let the boys down like that, though, can I? Not when this has all been my idea in the first place. But the words won't come out. I can't say it. I'm stuck, and this time it isn't just my stammer. I can't speak *and* I can't think properly.

The floppy-haired boy walks past us in the doorway and says, "Have a think about it. I know it's not easy, but we could really do with someone like you. We're gonna do some paid gigs soon too, so you know, it would be like a *proper* band. When are you next rehearsing?" he says, looking up at the schedule.

"Wednesday," I whisper.

"Great, well, you can tell us then," and he winks at me, shrugs an apology at the others and slinks off down the hall.

The rehearsal feels a bit weird after that. The excitement we'd felt has vanished and we all seem a bit miserable. When we start playing it sounds like we have never even picked up our instruments before. It's awful. I look up, hoping that no one is laughing at the terrible noise we're making.

After ten minutes of getting nowhere and no one

saying anything, Alex stands up and asks, "What are you going to do, Billy? There is no point us even being here if you are just going to join them anyway."

"Yeah," adds Matthew. "It does seem a bit stupid to practise if we don't know that you are staying with us."

I look at Josh and he's looking down at the floor like he wants to sink into it. *I can't do it to them*, I think, *I started this so I should finish it and they are my friends after all. The first proper friends I have ever had.*

"Of c-c-c-course I'm sticking with you guys," I say as lightly as possible, trying to make it sound like I hadn't even considered ditching them. The truth is that for the rest of the day and night I can't stop thinking about being the drummer for Teenplay.

The next morning, after everyone has headed off to lessons, I ask Mr Osho what he would do.

"Gosh, that's a tricky one, isn't it, buddy? Only you know how committed you are to the boys. Have you chatted to them about it?"

"N-Not really. I told them I was staying."

"Why did you tell them that?"

"I didn't want to upset them. They are my mates."

"Well, maybe there's your answer."

"I know b-but I couldn't stop thinking about it. I had a d-d-dream last night that I was a drummer for Teenplay and we were playing at W-Wembley."

"Ha! So now you don't know what to do? Friendship versus fame and fortune."

"Kind of."

"Sometimes, when I can't decide on something important, I find it useful to imagine looking in at myself as if I'm not involved, as if I'm just flying above the whole situation, or like it's a TV show. Then I can picture me making both choices and how they may play out, decide which person I want to be, what I want my story to be. Does that make any sense?"

"Yeah, I guess."

On my way to French I start imagining me telling the boys that I'm leaving and how sad they'd be. I picture Josh crying and Alex not knowing what to say. I picture me in lessons on my own, feeling lonely like I used to. Then another picture forms, an image from my dream, of people clapping in a huge audience and everyone chanting, "TEENPLAY! TEENPLAY! TEENPLAY!"

I don't know who I want to be. Can't I be both? A good friend *and* the drummer in a different band?

I spend most of the day avoiding the boys. I feel

like they will see my thoughts and know in a second that a huge part of me wants to ditch them. Me and Skyla spend lunchtime together, but she knows that something's wrong,

"I think I prefer Billy the comedian to Billy the grumpy drummer," she says over her chips. "Are you planning on saying anything this lunch?"

"Sorry that I'm n-not always in a good mood, OK?" I get up, ditch my tray and go and find my spot under the stairs, where I used to hide from Blakemore. This time I'm trying to hide from everyone. I just don't know what to do.

By the time Wednesday lunchtime comes, I am in an even worse state. I must have changed my mind a thousand times. Every time I think I'm sure, and that I'm going to do the right thing and just stay with my friends, I think about how good Teenplay are. My thoughts are whizzing, they're drowning out everything else, so that it's hard to concentrate. As I'm staring out of the window in geography I get told off by Mr Grant.

"Bobby! Will you stop daydreaming, please!" He still doesn't know my name.

I don't get any work done in maths at all.

"This is not like you, Billy," Mr Randall says when

he sees my blank book. It's almost a relief when the bell goes for lunch. A part of me hopes that the other band aren't even there or have totally forgotten that they asked me in the first place. When we get to the Music Lounge I feel completely miserable when I see them packing away. The floppy-haired boy looks up and waves in my direction and immediately says, "So are you joining us, drummer boy? What's your name anyway?"

"B-B-B-B-Billy."

"OK, B-B-Billy. Who you gonna drum for?" As he says this the drummer/keyboard player starts a low drum roll just to add pressure.

Everyone in the room is looking now.

I glance at Alex, who's smiling at me, and then towards Teenplay. I keep looking between the two groups, panic rising in my chest. I can see Mr Osho watching from his desk. I try my hardest to find some words, to say, "Sorry, I can't," when I see Ellie chatting with a group of Year Twelves on the other side of the Music Lounge. I remember how much she'd liked Teenplay. How she'd whistled with her fingers for them.

I start again to imagine my life if I were in *their* band. My thoughts start to get loud inside my head.

You would be hanging out with Ellie every lunchtime. Walking down the corridors and all the older kids waving at you. Everyone cheering you on. Everyone knowing who you are, but not because of your stammer. Blakemore wouldn't pick on you any more if you were surrounded by Year Twelves, nobody would pick on you any more. Rock is way cooler than jazz. Maybe this is it. This is the moment that your life will change. Maybe this is who you are meant to be.

Then it happens.

"YES," I say, my eyes still on Ellie. I look back to the floppy-haired boy and say, "Yes, I will be the drummer in Teenplay." I try my hardest not to look at Alex, Josh and Matthew. I also don't want to look at Mr Osho either, even though I only did what he told me to do. To decide what kind of person I want to be.

It gets awkward instantly and after the biggest silence of my life Alex says, "It's fine, Billy, I don't blame you. We're not as good as these guys," but he doesn't look at me when he says it, and his eyes are kind of sad.

"I didn't even want to do the stupid talent show in the first place," Matthew adds and half-heartedly pats me on the back. When I glance at Josh, he's really annoyed and he doesn't even try and hide it like the others.

"You sure, kid?" says the boy with the floppy hair. "I don't want to cause any arguments between band members, bro."

I could change my mind and stick with the boys. They have been good friends to me. The first friends I have ever really had. I remember my sleepover and laughing in the garage. It was so much fun and it all felt so easy. But an offer like this is massive, isn't it? If I can't be a comedian any more, then maybe I should start taking drumming seriously, and Teenplay are *really* good. The boys will get over it. They'll still be my friends.

"Yes," I say, nodding my head, but feeling instantly sick in my stomach.

"Well, that's just brilliant," Josh shouts. "I thought we were mates, Billy! We were only doing this because of you."

"Can't you guys s-s-s-still d-d-do it?" I mumble, knowing that a band without a drummer is not really a band.

"Thanks for nothing, you idiot," he says and storms off. I instantly feel like I have made a massive mistake as the others kind of shrug and follow him.

"Welcome to the band, kid. You won't regret it!"

says floppy-haired boy, but I feel like I already do.

Josh hasn't really spoken to me since. The others pretend to be OK but I know they're not. It's all changed. In form class last week I asked if they wanted to come over for tea, and they all said they were busy. I don't think they *were* busy.

They say hi and I still sit with them but they talk about stuff I don't know about. Games they are playing at lunchtimes. It feels like they do it on purpose. Once, when they were talking about something that happened in the lunch queue, Josh said, "You wouldn't know about that, though, Billy, you're probably too busy with your new band to care."

He really loved playing the box bass. That's why he is so upset. I think it was the first thing that he found where his constant jiggling actually helped him. They could just do the show without me. Find a new drummer, for goodness' sake. I think it's a bit pathetic. I think they are just jealous. Any one of them would have made the same decision. I'll be fine without them. Won't I?

So that's my life now. I'm the drummer in my new band. TEENPLAY. It's a bit of a daft name as I'm not even a teenager yet! They all are. They call the music we play "indie", but I don't really know what that is. I think it just sounds like the stuff me and Dad play in the garage. At the moment Teenplay mainly do covers but we want to start writing our own songs too.

My favourite is "Mardy Bum" by Arctic Monkeys, there's a section where the drums really kick in and I love it. The others say I'm "off the hook", whatever that means. I think it's a good thing.

The singer and guitarist, Sam, is the leader. He's the one with the floppy hair. He has a girlfriend. I've seen them on the field holding hands. I must have been staring as I saw her whisper to him and he looked over at me and waved. Then they both started laughing.

The bass guitarist, Phoebe, is a girl, but she says she doesn't really want to be. She has short black hair and her school blazer is really big. Everyone calls her P.

The drummer with the pink cheeks who's now back on the keyboards is called Ollie. He's definitely better on the keyboard. Ollie's super nice. He only learned the drums because their old drummer left the band. The old drummer kept getting really mad and shouting all the time so they had a vote and sacked him.

Mum says that I have become "moody" since

joining Teenplay. She says that I'm her little "mardy bum". It really annoys me when she says that. Dad laughs like he's totally on her side. I'm not "mardy". They just don't understand. I don't need to talk to her about every little thing that's happening to me like I used to. She thinks that means I'm being rude, but I don't think that's fair. She says it's "a real shame" that I'm not with The Regulars any more. "They were such lovely boys." That makes me really mad.

Meanwhile, William Blakemore hasn't got me for ages. Today in our maths session I brought loads of Lego in for us to use and he brought some Minecraft characters. We ended up not doing much maths and just messing about, building stuff, but Mr Osho didn't seem to mind.

I can't get used to Blakemore not being so horrible. Like maybe it's all a trick and he is just messing with my head. I'm still convinced he will jump out from behind every door, be waiting in every corridor, and when he isn't, it puts me on edge. Like the scene in a scary movie, where waiting for the shock is worse than the actual moment. It feels like I am always waiting for something bad to happen. I am just never sure what the next thing will be.

CHAPTER 25

I have no friends but I love my shoes.
They are my sole companions.

The smell of cooking and rot as I walk into The Oaks is even stronger than normal. I've brought some ratatouille that I made in food tech. Granny Bread loves trying what I make each week. She tastes it and pretends to be one of the judges on *MasterChef*. Her favourite so far is the fish pie. I'm holding the foil tub and three plastic spoons, in case Mrs Gibbens wants some too, and listening to a new song that we are trying to learn for the talent show.

I know something is wrong when I look up and see Mum talking to one of the nurses in the hallway outside Granny Bread's door. Mum never comes to visit in the afternoon, this is my slot. Time slows as she looks at me with red eyes and a sad mouth. She opens up her arms. "It was a big one this time," she whispers as I take off my headphones.

I freeze. She hugs me. I can feel her really shaking hard as she squeezes me. I know that she definitely isn't crying with relief or happiness this time. This is a different cry. One that I've never seen before, and one that I will never forget.

Granny Bread died today.

CHAPTER 26

Why did the banana go to the doctors?
He was peeling really bad.

I remember the way she looked at me when she first moved into The Oaks. Scared. The Oaks care home felt like somewhere people go to die. So that's what she did. I should have *done* something. When she looked at me like that, asking me to help her with her eyes, I should have tried harder. Begged for her to come home with us. Not stopped. Then maybe she would not have looked so scared and she would be here right now, squeezing my hand and listening to me read to her. I don't say this to Mum, obviously. Not to anyone.

I keep picturing Granny Bread. Pulling her funny face behind Mum's back when she was moaning about the drum kit being too loud. Doing an impression of a Dumbo octopus. Laughing at one of my jokes, head back and hand on her chest. It makes me smile. When I catch myself smiling, I feel bad. Like smiling and laughing are wrong now. Does that mean smiling will feel bad for ever?

The day after it happens, Mum knocks on my door and sits on the end of my bed. I'm reading a fact book called *Amazing Animals*. Reading seems OK. Appropriate. There are some things that I *can* do and some things I *can't*. I like to separate them. To make it clear to myself, what I'm allowed to do. I'm making a list for my pinboard. *Smiling = BAD. Laughing = BAD. Reading = GOOD.*

I've been doing a lot of reading. It means I don't have to see anyone or do any more "talking". That's all they want me to do. Talk about how I'm feeling. Well, the problem with that is I don't really know how I'm "feeling". All I know is it's not nice, so I don't really want to talk about it.

The thing I really don't want to say, not to anyone, ever, is that I'm scared that I'll never find anyone who makes my stammer go away like Granny Bread did. The reason I can't say it is because it sounds silly and selfish. Like the only reason I loved Granny Bread is because I didn't stammer so much when I was with her. Even thinking about it is making me feel like a bad person, because it's not true. Not at all. I loved her for loads of reasons.

1. For always being pleased to see me.
2. For playing patience with me.
3. For being so funny.
4. For the way she claps her hands when she listens to her cassette tapes.
5. For loving *Blue Planet* even more than I do.
6. For saying things that are inappropriate.
7. For laughing at my jokes.
8. For loving me so much.

So why do I keep thinking about my stupid stammer? My brain is stuck on the stammer channel.

Thinking about my stammer = BAD.

Mum sits on my bed for a while, as I pretend to read, not saying anything. She has a shoebox. It's a Nike shoebox and so I think maybe she has bought me some trainers to cheer me up. It almost works. I start to imagine what colour they might be. Maybe they're the same as Matthew's. He's got the coolest trainers; they start light blue and then go darker blue towards the top and they have a gold tick. Thinking of Matthew's trainers just makes me feel worse. I wish I could see them – The Regulars. I really miss them. Especially now.

Then she taps the box gently and says, "I brought you some bits and pieces of Granny Bread's. Things that she kept. I thought you would want them." Then I feel really bad. Why am I thinking about stupid trainers?

Imagining new trainers = BAD.

She gives me a hug. She is hugging me so much I feel like I'm suffocating. I don't stop her, though, I think it's more for her than for me. I watched her crying as she was doing the washing up yesterday. She didn't know I was there. I snuck down and peeked in through the gap in the door. Tears were falling down her face while she was staring out of the window, her hands still in the water. It was weird, like she wasn't really crying and she didn't even notice, but the tears were just coming out. So I let her hug me for as long as she wants because I know she feels so bad.

Letting Mum hug me = GOOD.

I'm not opening the shoebox. The idea of opening it makes my chest hurt so that I can't breathe. But it's just sitting there in the corner, looking at me. I try to focus on my book but I can't read the words or look at the pictures. Not while the box is there. I try a different book but my eyes still keep going back to the Nike tick. Wondering what's inside. I pick up a towel from the floor and throw it over the box, but it just makes it worse. It looks even bigger somehow. I shake my head and take a big breath in. I can't ignore it any more. I'm going to look in it.

There are loads of pictures in it. Things that I have drawn for Granny Bread and notes that I've written. Things from when I was really little. She's kept it all.

Dear Granny,

I love you so much. You are the best granny in the world. Thank you for the Lego. I love it.

Love from Billy.

(Age 6)

This one was from before she became Granny Bread. I don't know why I put my age on it; she knew how old I was. Imagine if everyone put their age on letters and emails.

Dear Mr Robson,

I read your letter with interest and will
respond in due course.
Kind Regards
Malcolm Miggins
(Age 49)

There it is again. My smile. That bad feeling. Writing joke letters = BAD.

There are so many things to look at in the box. Drawings of sharks, a handprint from when I was two, thank-you notes, a drawing of an octopus, a photo of me and her outside her old flat, smiling, her arm around my shoulder. And at the bottom there is a little tiny bottle of shells, tied with a white ribbon. I bought them with my holiday money when we went to Spain. I thought she would want something from the sea in her little flat. A tear rolled down her cheek when I gave them to her and she said she would "treasure them for ever".

I don't want them. I don't want any of it. They're not mine. It's wrong that they're in my bedroom. They aren't mine! They were hers. They should be with her.

I shove everything back into the box and sellotape it round and round until I run out of tape. I don't know what to do with it then but I know I need it to be out of my hands. I start feeling panicky and my chest feels tight and so I open the wardrobe and shove it as far back as I can and cover it with all my winter coats. I slam the wardrobe door shut as though there's a ghost inside. I sit on my bed and breathe in through my nose and out through my mouth like Sue tells me to when I'm feeling stressed. I can feel my heart beating hard in my chest. Nothing is going to be the same any more, without Granny Bread. Why did she have to die?

Then a photograph lying on the carpet catches my eye. It must have fallen out of the box. It's a faded picture of a little dog looking up towards the camera with loads of fuzzy black fur and its tongue hanging out. I turn over the photograph and see in scrawled tiny handwriting: *My darling Scraggles.* Mrs Gibbens must have given it to Granny Bread. I'm not sure why Mum put it in the box.

I carefully pin the photo up on my pinboard and stare at it for ages, remembering what Granny Bread had said: *She's got no one. No one that would bother.* Then I picture Granny Bread's face and feel bad for even thinking about stupid Scraggles.

Thinking about cute dogs = BAD.

I've not been back into my wardrobe for three

days; I don't want to catch a glimpse of the box. When Mum asks why I'm wearing the same clothes again and tells me, "Go and get changed. You're too old to wear the same clothes for days on end. You'll stink!" I can't tell her the truth, so I go upstairs and open the wardrobe door the tiniest bit and stick just my arm in and grab the first thing I feel. Mum looks a bit funny when I come down in last year's Christmas jumper, but she doesn't say anything.

I have to go back to school tomorrow. Mum let me have Thursday and Friday off last week but she says, "You have to get back to normal. It'll probably help." I don't know how I can, when everything is so different. I feel so different. I just want to hide from everyone and everything.

CHAPTER 27

A kid threw a lump of cheese at me.
It wasn't very mature.

When one bad thing happens it feels like other bad things see their chance and start happening too. Even the weather seems to know how I feel and wants to make it worse. The sky is dark and it hasn't stopped raining for five days. I feel like I'm outside of myself. Walking around school on my own, not really feeling anything. Like a zombie.

Today in English I have to read out loud. Mrs Timpson the English teacher always makes us read out loud when we start a new book. We're reading *Great Expectations*. It's really thick. It's got more than four hundred pages. It's about a boy who wants to go to London and change his life. I wish I could go to London and change my life.

She's never picked on me before, which I thought was really kind. But she must be in a bad mood today, like me. Maybe it's catching and I gave her the bad mood.

I begin OK and then get *really* stuck on the word "Pip".

"P-P-P-P-P-P-P-P-P-P-P-P-P-P-P-P-P-P-P-P—"

Then I just have a total block. A block is where no sound at all will come out. It feels like I'm in a bear trap and the more I fight against it the tighter it gets. My eyes are clamping shut and my jaw is jutting out. I feel totally out of control. Eventually I just move on to the next word.

The main character is called Pip so I know I'm in trouble. Every time I can see the word coming up it gets worse and worse.

"So I called myself P-P-P-P-P-P-P-P-P-P-P-P-P-P-P-P-P-P-P-P-P-P-P-P-Piiiip, and came t-t-to be caaaalled P-P-P-P-P-P-P-P-P-P-P-P-P-P-P-P-P-Piiip."

Everyone starts giggling. I can see that they are all looking ahead to find the "Pip"s.

Mrs Timpson pretends she can't hear all the laughing and makes me carry on for ages. Alex, Josh and Matthew just put their heads down and avoid looking at me. Skyla just keeps looking and waiting, with a sad smile. It's bad. I just want to go home. Go home and never see any of them ever again.

Afterwards in the corridor all the girls are huddled up whispering. I assume they are talking about me and then Kai Daniels pretends to bump into me and says, "Sorry, P-P-Pip." All the girls laugh.

A few of them start calling me Pip all the time. Even some of the girls. Sophie asks to borrow a rubber in art and when I give her one she says, "Thanks, Pip." Then creases up like it's the funniest thing ever.

I didn't realize that things could actually get any worse. I start thinking about Sue and wonder if she is on the beach.

On Wednesday, it's like Blakemore is actually getting worse at algebra. I ask him a question that he got right the week before and he can't do it at all this week. It's really annoying. I can't teach him anything new as he forgets everything from before. I'm glad I don't have his brain, it must be really frustrating.

When I say this to him he slams his book down and says, "Well, I'm glad I haven't got your stupid brain, P-P-Pip," and storms out. I feel a bit bad then.

Mr Osho looks up from his marking. "What

happened there, Billy? You two seemed to be getting on."

Blakemore has been leaving me alone recently. Thinking about it, even when I was getting stuck on *Great Expectations* he didn't join in with the others, he looked a bit angry if anything.

"I d-d-don't know why I said it, sir," I say.

"What did you say to him, Billy?"

"Th-That I w-wouldn't want his brain."

"Oh, I see."

"I d-d-don't know what's wrong w-w-with me, s-s-sir. I'm upsetting everyone."

"That's not like you at all, Billy, is it?"

I shake my head and put my face in my hands.

Mr Osho continues, "Sometimes when things are getting too much, we take it out on the people nearest to us, even if it's not on purpose. Everyone does it, Billy. It's what you do from now that matters."

"I don't know what to do. I never know what to do," I sob into my hands.

"You've had a lot going on, buddy. Don't be too hard on yourself."

"I just can't do anything right."

"You will get yourself back on track, I have no doubt about that. Sometimes it just takes a bit of time," he says, and as I sit there wondering what the right track is and whether I'll ever be happy again, the bell goes and kids start pouring into the classroom so I have to wipe my eyes and get to French.

I nearly go over and say sorry to Blakemore but he doesn't look up and so I just walk straight past his desk. Maybe I don't need to say sorry anyway. I mean, after all of the things he's done to me in the past, it's not like I'm the bad guy, is it?

At lunchtime the band are arguing. When Sam stomps into rehearsal he's in a terrible mood and is playing really badly. Then when he forgets the lyrics, he shouts, "I don't want to be in this stupid band any more. What's the point?"

Ollie just makes it worse. "Come on, mate, I know you and Tia have split up, but don't take it out on us!" He grins.

Sam turns on him. "It's got nothing to do with that! You haven't got a clue what you're talking about. It's this stupid band. We're nowhere near ready for the show. Look at us. We've got a loser on the bass and a little kid who can't even speak on the drums. We should be called The Weirdos."

No one in the band has ever mentioned my stammer before so I had kind of tricked myself into thinking that they hadn't even noticed. That's the whole point of being a drummer, so that no one notices me.

I go red and try to hide my face by looking down at my sticks. I can feel something in my tummy building up. P is looking at the floor too. Ollie gets really cross then.

"That's not on, Sam. You're making everyone feel bad. Look at them," he says, pointing at me and P. "Go and sort yourself out." Sam takes his guitar and storms out of the room.

As the door closes I see a face looking through the little round window. It takes me a moment to realize who it is. Ellie! Why did she have to come *now*?! Why couldn't she have seen any other rehearsal? It's so unfair. I want to rewind and change everything. This is not how things are meant to be. It's not part of the plan. But when I look back up at the window she's gone.

Ollie tells us not to worry about it. He says that Sam will be over it in a few days, but it's too late. The feeling in my tummy has moved into my chest; it feels so tight like I can't breathe and am being squashed. Suddenly out of nowhere, it comes out. Sick. I'm sick all over the drums, all over my sticks and my uniform and everything.

Ollie shouts, "Oh my god, Billy!" and P moves away. She looks disgusted.

Some kids shout from the beanbags, "Erggh, Pip's vommed," and then start making retching noises.

I throw my sticks down and run. Down the hall, past Ellie and her friends and out of the door. I carry on until I'm breathing hard and kind of fall on to the grass by the tennis courts.

"I hate it!" I scream into the rain and the wind. "I don't want to be me any more," I sob into the grass. "I don't want to be Billy Plimpton any more." I keep saying it over and over again. "I don't want to be Billy Plimpton." Until I feel a hand on my back.

It's Ellie.

She just sits down on the wet grass next to me and doesn't say anything. Eventually I wipe my face and sit up and we both stare at the empty tennis courts for what seems like for ever.

"It's crap sometimes, isn't it?" she says.

I just nod and wipe my nose with my sicky sleeve. I don't really care that she's seeing me like this. I don't really care about anything any more.

"My dad always says, 'If you just keep putting one foot in front of the other, and keep your chin up, eventually the view changes.'" Then she puts her arm around my shoulder and leans her head on to mine and I ever so slightly feel the view begin to change.

CHAPTER 28

Sometimes I tuck my knees into my chest and lean forward.
That's just how I roll.

I have been putting one foot in front of the other and it has got me here. This is what the view looks like now.

Ollie was right. Sam came back to rehearsal two days later and we've started practising again. It doesn't feel right any more. It's awkward. P feels the same, I can tell. She looks even more embarrassed than she normally does. I really miss playing board games with Alex, Josh and Matthew. Now they just look up at me rehearsing every now and then, but look away every time I catch them. Even Skyla seems to be chatting to me less. When she found out about me ditching The Regulars, she said, "Wow, that's not like you."

"Well, maybe I want to be d-d-d-different," I said.

"You are different, Billy. You've not told me a joke for weeks. Are you OK?"

"Yeah, of course I am. I'm in T-T-T-Teenplay!"

"OK," she said and walked off down the hall.

I feel really lonely all the time now, even though I've got the band. I *really, really* miss Granny Bread. I have a constant weird feeling in my tummy all the time and I'm always worried I might be sick again. I'm trying my hardest to ignore it, and just trying to keep putting the next foot down and keep my chin up.

After school I decide to walk past The Oaks, I don't know why. Maybe I think it might bring me closer to Granny Bread again. Make me feel less lonely. As I'm looking up at the red bricks and the neat grass outside I see a face peering out of one of the ground floor windows, waving at me. For a tiny second I think it's Granny Bread and then I look again and see Mrs Gibbens. She looks pleased to see me and I know that she has been sitting there all day, every day, just like Granny Bread said. Hoping to see Scraggles. As I'm waving back at her I picture Scraggles' face looking out from my pinboard and I head over to her window. By the time I get there she's managed to open it and has her scrawny arm reached out towards me.

"Billy! You poor love," she says as she grabs on to my hand. "We all miss her so much." She has tears welled up in her eyes. "You poor, poor love. I know what it's like to miss someone, Billy. It's not fair, is it?"

"N-N-No it's n-n-not fair," I say, trying to ignore the tight feeling in my throat that's stopping me from swallowing.

"She was the closest thing I had to family, since Scraggles. She really was a lovely woman, so kind. Come and see me, Billy, whenever you want. I would love that."

In this moment, I know exactly what I need to do.

I promise Mrs Gibbens that I will come back and see her and then I run. I run home as fast as I can and head straight upstairs to my room.

"What are you doing rushing around, Billy? I've not seen you move this fast for weeks," Mum says as I dash back downstairs holding the photo in my hands.

"I have to find this dog," I say, catching my breath.

"What are you on about? Whose dog is it?"

"It doesn't matter. How would you find a missing dog?"

"You are not bringing a dog back here, Billy. We have talked about this before, there is absolutely no way..." But I can't hear the rest of it as I'm grabbing my bag and out of the door too fast.

On my way to the library I wonder if I should ask Skyla to help me, but I don't really think she's my friend any more so I decide that this is something I'll have to do on my own. When I get there I ask to use the photocopier and a man with a bald head comes and helps me. I only have one pound in my wallet which won't get me many copies, but it's a start.

"OK, what are we copying today?" he asks. When I hand over the photograph he says, "What a cutie pie! Only trouble is, the colour is so dark and faded it's unlikely to come out that well. Shall we give it a go and see?"

I nod and watch as the bright light flashes and moves across the photograph. The paper that slides out is useless, you can't see Scraggles at all, it's just dark fuzzy blackness. My shoulders slump and I let out a big sigh.

"Don't worry, fella, we will figure something out. What's it for?"

"My g-g-g-granny's f-f-f-f-friend has l-l-l-lost her dog."

"Aw, and you're trying to find it?"

"Yes. I wwas g-g-g-g-going to make a p-p-poster."

"Have you tried the RSPCA or the rehoming centres?"

"No," I say, perking up.

"Well, have a little google and you can give them a call. I know there is one called Millbrook not far from here but there may be others. I'm sure you will find him. Good luck!"

I make a list of seven different places that I can try. I start with the RSPCA and as I take out my phone from my bag I nearly stop myself and just email them instead. Using the phone is still my number one nightmare! I can't hang around waiting for emails, though, that could take weeks. I need to talk to someone now.

"H-H-H-Hello, I'm l-l-l-l-l-l-looking for a d-d-d-d-d-d-d-d-d-dog," I begin.

Eventually after what feels like the longest call ever I put the phone down. No Scraggles there. When I get down to number six on the list I'm losing hope but the phone calls weirdly are getting easier each time I make them,

"Hello, Millbrook Dogs and Cats Home," says an incredibly chirpy voice.

"H-Hello, I'm l-looking f-for a d-dog," I say.

"When did your dog go missing?" says the voice, now sounding full of concern.

Ten minutes later, I'm running in the direction of Millbrook Dogs and Cats Home, clutching the photograph. The lady said that a few months ago a dog was found which sounds like it could have been Scraggles.

"Bring the photograph in and we can see if it is a match."

"OK," I said. "I'll come now."

"We close in half an hour so be as quick as you can!"

I end up completely lost and running twice round a housing estate before I see the sign with a picture of a dog and a cat on it. By the time I run through the doors they are just about to close and I am sweating and exhausted.

"You made it!" says the chirpy voice from the phone and I look up to see a lady with thick glasses and her hair all wrapped up in a colourful headscarf, smiling at me from the reception desk. When I show her the picture she immediately grins and says, "That's him all right, what a sweet boy he was."

"Was?" I ask.

"Yes," she says, looking through her glasses with eyes full of worry. *Oh no*, I think, *please don't let him have died, how would I tell Mrs Gibbens?* Then she continues, "We hold the dogs for four weeks, in case their owners are looking for them, and after that time we put them up for adoption. In this case it took no time at all for us to find his forever home. He really was a sweetie, we were sad to see him go."

"B-But w-w-what about Mrs G-Gibbens?" I say. "She misses him s-s-s-so much."

"Mrs Gibbens is your granny's friend, yes?" I nod, wondering what to do. What was I even hoping for? She can't have him back anyway, The Oaks would never allow it and the new owners won't want to give him up. All of a sudden I feel really young and stupid for not having thought about it all properly. I put my head in my hands.

"How about I get us some juice and biscuits and you can tell me all about it and then we can make a plan? Sound good?" I nod and try to smile.

"My name is Patsy Arnold," she says, holding out her hand.

"My name is Billy Plimpton," I say as I shake it.

CHAPTER 29

Sheepdog: All forty sheep accounted for, sir.
Farmer: But I only have thirty-six sheep.
Sheepdog: I rounded them up, sir.

We got the *Bannerdale's Got Talent Show* line-up yesterday. It was posted on the pinboard outside the dinner hall. We are on right at the end, straight after Molly Hollwell. She's in my food tech class. She's really short and has hair so long that she can sit on it. She is dancing with her dog. There are no other bands playing, only people singing with backing tracks, which is a bit rubbish in my opinion. There are lots of dancers, a magician and a contortionist. There are no comedians. I checked. As the only band we will make a big impression.

On my way to our last rehearsal I see Ellie. She's

walking down the corridor towards me. I want to turn and run the other way but she's already waving. I've not seen her since the sick and the view of the tennis courts.

"Hi, Billy! Just the boy I want to see."

"R-R-Really?"

"Yes. I saw the talent show line-up and saw that you're still doing it? I just wanted to find you to say good luck!"

"Oh, wow. OK."

"Good luck!" and with a wave she's gone, her red hair bouncing up the corridor.

The whole school is coming to the show and everyone's getting really excited, talking about it non-stop.

I can't believe it's tomorrow. There's going to be a raffle stall and Christmas crêpes made with lemon, sugar and cloves. The art department is making a big backdrop with stars all over it. The local news are coming to film it again and Dad is the cameraman!

Everyone in the band is wearing Christmas jumpers, and after school Mum takes me shopping to get mine. We go jumper shopping every year, it's kind of like a tradition of ours now, I suppose. She wants me to get a stupid knitted Christmas tree with pom-poms all over it but I say, "No way." There is nothing rock and roll about a pom-pom. I get a black jumper with a silver T-rex in a red Santa hat on it. I think it's pretty good for a Christmas jumper. Chloe gets a pink one with a reindeer on it. In my opinion pink is not a Christmas colour, but Chloe doesn't listen. She keeps telling me to shut up, until Mum uses her whispery-angry voice on us. "Neither is black, Billy! Just leave your sister alone."

After that we go for hot chocolate and Mum asks if we want to go and see Santa in his grotto. I say, "No!" but Chloe is desperate, so I have to queue for half an hour to see some sad-looking elves and a pretend Father Christmas in a tiny room covered in cotton wool. He asks what we want for Christmas and obviously Chloe says a pony. She has asked for a pony every year since she was three. She doesn't seem to get that it's never going to happen.

When he asks me, "What about you, young man? What's on your Christmas list?" I want to tell him that we are just here for my sister, and that I'm too old, but I feel bad so tell him I want a record player and some vinyl. He says, "Wow, no one has ever asked me for that before! You're a cool little kid. I'll definitely try and get you that!" He doesn't sound like Father

Christmas at all, he has a Scottish accent and I can see a tattoo on his arm under his baggy red sleeve, but I don't really mind.

On our way home, Mum whispers, "Thanks for going to the grotto. I know you're too old for it all now."

"That's all right, Mum. I kind of enjoyed it." And I did, I wasn't lying. It was nice to be out with Mum and Chloe. To do the same thing that we do every year. It felt safe, like nothing really changes. Even when it feels like everything has. On the way back on the bus, my phone rings and I see Millbrook's number pop up.

"Hi, P-Patsy," I say, trying to keep Mum and Chloe from hearing, but I can already see them pulling faces at me. When Patsy tells me that everything is set, and that the plan is on, I whisper, "Brilliant. I'll see you there."

Two hours later I'm standing round the corner from The Oaks, jiggling up and down to try and stay warm. I got here a bit early to check that Mrs Gibbens was looking out of her window as usual. Sure enough, when I peek round the hedge I can just make out her sad face. I'm getting excited now. It feels great to be doing something that will make her so happy.

I can hear snuffling as Patsy and Scraggles head up the road towards me. Scraggles immediately starts pulling at the lead to sniff my legs and rub his fuzzy little body against me.

"Hello, Scraggles!" I say, and he looks at me with his funny squashed-up face and I instantly know why Mrs Gibbens loves him so much. "Hello, boy. You are about to make someone very happy. Yes, you are!"

"I told you he's a sweetheart!" Patsy says, laughing as Scraggles starts licking my face. "So the owners have said every Thursday at this time, if that works for you?"

"Yeah, it's perfect," I say.

"It is perfect. They needed someone to walk him anyway and when I told them the story it just about broke their hearts, and so fingers crossed this will make everyone happy. Including you, Mr Scraggles," she says, as she ruffles the fur on his neck. "So, is she there?"

"Yes, all set. Let's go!" and Patsy hands me the lead.

When Mrs Gibbens first sees us I have a bit of panic that we may have given her another heart attack. She puts her hands to the glass and I can see her mouth forming the word, "Scraggles," over and over again as the tears start streaming down her wrinkly cheeks. She vanishes from the window and we make our way to the entrance, knowing that she's on her way.

Scraggles goes completely nuts when he sees her and pulls the lead so hard that it slips out of my hand and he manages to get through the doors and into the reception. Mrs Gibbens ends up on the floor with Scraggles on top of her, licking her perfectly made-up face while she giggles like a little girl.

"I'm never going to be able to get up from here, am I, Billy? It's hard enough getting off the sofa!"

When we tell her the plan, and that she can see Scraggles every week, she grabs hold of my hand and says,

"Billy, your granny always told me what an amazing boy you are. I just wish she was here to see this, I really do."

"Me too," I say.

As I look at Mrs Gibbens sitting on the floor stroking Scraggles's scruffy fur I wonder how I could have ever been scared of her.

"I tell you what, seeing you and this scruff bag once a week, that'll change my life, that will. Thank you so much." Then she grabs my hand and kisses Scraggles again and again and keeps saying, "Thank you, thank you, thank you." Over and over. As we sit there, I hold on to Mrs Gibbens's wrinkled hand and look up at Patsy smiling down at us and feel really good, for the first time in a long time.

CHAPTER 30

I wrote a song about a tortilla.
Actually it's more of a rap.

We're going to play two songs. "Mardy Bum" and a song we've just learned called "Smells like Teen Spirit" by Nirvana. Sam picked it because he thought it went with our name, Teenplay. P refuses to wear any kind of Christmas jumper, so she is in her normal baggy black clothes and is just going to put some tinsel on her bass guitar. Now that I'm here, I can't wait until it's done. Then school will be over for a bit.

As we wait in the corridor backstage, I peek through the curtains at the audience. Ellie is in the second row with her dad. Mum and Chloe are a few rows further back. There are so many people! It looks like thousands. It's really loud. Mr Osho is standing at the side with Mrs Able. I start thinking about the people who I can't see. I scan each row. So many faces that I don't know, and who don't know me. I can't find Alex or Josh. I can see Matthew's head high above the rest. Skyla is standing at the back, her hair looks like it's been brushed. Then I keep looking and for a second I think I've seen Granny Bread.

Molly is just about to start. Her dog doesn't look very well trained to me. She keeps shouting at him and eventually he runs to the front of the stage and does a wee by the microphone. Everyone's laughing now. The laughter is really loud and doesn't sound very nice. Molly tells off the little dog and picks him up. She takes a bow but no one claps and then she comes offstage looking really flustered.

A couple of Year Thirteens who have been sorting out all the props push past me and run on with some kitchen roll and the audience cheer. They sound a bit wild. They have been sitting there for two hours. I think they're bored.

That's when it all happens. Sam is standing outside the fire door into the car park. I just assume he's nervous or doing a warm-up or something. Me, Ollie and P are all kind of pacing around not really knowing what to say to each other. I have a final look through the door and see the props guys taking my drums through the curtains and on to the stage.

"Any minute," I whisper to Ollie. Then we hear the fire door slam shut and turn to see Sam standing behind us. He has his phone in his hand and looks furious.

"How could you do that to me?" he hisses at Ollie. Ollie seems to instantly know what he's talking about and just shrugs and puts his head down. He looks guilty, but I have no idea why. I feel really confused and Sam looks different. Like an animal.

Sam pushes him then, in the chest, hard, and Ollie nearly falls over. I'm really scared. I'm shaking and I don't know why Sam's so angry, but most of all I want to protect Ollie. I stand in between them.

"C-C-C-Calm down, SAAM!" I stammer, but Sam isn't listening and shoves me to one side as he comes towards Ollie, who's still off balance.

Then Sam hits him. Hard. In the face.

I have never seen anyone actually be punched in the face before. I can hear the dull slap of Sam's fist. I'll never forget it. It feels really scary. Ollie holds his head in his hands and I scream at Sam, "Leave him alone!! Leave us alone! OK?"

Sam kicks the wall. I think he must have broken his foot he kicks it so hard. He limps off through the fire door and rips down a poster on his way.

Ollie looks at me and P sheepishly and shrugs his shoulders. "Sorry, guys," he apologizes. "Thanks for sticking up for me, little man!" Then he ruffles my hair and heads off down the corridor, catching the blood from his nose in his hand.

I have no idea what's going on. I look at P, who just stares at the floor and mumbles, "I think that means Ollie's going out with Tia, which means the end of the band. Soz, Bill." And with that she shuffles off after Ollie.

My heart's racing and I'm sweating. I feel really awake. As I look through the door again I see the Year Thirteens putting the microphone in the middle of the stage. I only have the head teacher's introduction before Teenplay, a band that doesn't exist any more, will be announced. There's only me. I have absolutely no idea what to do.

Then I hear footsteps heading towards me. Alex is running down the corridor. "I just saw Ollie in the toilets, he was a mess. Are you OK?" I look at his face. He looks so worried. The fact he still cares about me makes my throat get tight and I think about it all at once.

Granny Bread. The pinky promise. The fact I have lost the best friends I ever made. William Blakemore. Everything.

Alex hugs me.

"I'm so sorry," I say once we've stopped. And then I look behind him and see Josh, Matthew and Skyla are there too.

"We wanted to wish you luck," Matthew says. "What's going on? Where are the others?"

"It's not happening," Alex tells them.

I look at them and whisper, "I have been a terrible friend." My eyes meet Josh's. "I'm really sorry."

He just shrugs and says, "We missed you. We missed you and your jokes. Now what are you going to do about this empty stage?"

Then Skyla takes something out of her back pocket. My joke book!

"How d-d-d-d-did you?"

"I saw your mum in the audience. She found it in the bin. She's worried about you too." Then as she passes it to me she says, "I think you should do it, Billy. Go up there and show the lot of them."

I take the joke book and nod. She gives me the biggest hug until my feet lift off the floor. "P-Put me down," I say, pretending to gasp for breath, "I c-c-can't b-b-breathe. Goodbye, one and all." They all laugh.

"He's back!" says Skyla and puts me down, and they all go to get back to their seats. I look on to the stage and then down the empty corridor. Two options. Two different directions for me to put one foot in front of the other one. Just then William Blakemore appears at the fire door, blocking one of my paths. He stands there, leaning against the wall, looking down at his shoes.

I open the joke book and inside the front cover is a little piece of paper with Mum's beautiful curly handwriting, it reads: *Remember, EVERYTHING you say is important.* I know what I have to do.

A face pops through the door and holds it open for me, giving me a thumbs up, and then I hear the head teacher say, "Welcome to the stage, our headline act of the evening, a band that is really going places... Teenplay!" The audience start clapping and I head towards the curtain. I can hear my footsteps loud on the wooden stage, in time with my heart beating hard in my chest. One foot in front of the other. As I'm taking my first steps, Blakemore says, "Billy?"

"Yeah?" I say, turning back to him.

"I'm sorry," he says.

"Me too."

"You know you don't have to do this if you don't want to?"

"I know."

He holds his hand out and I shake it.

The room falls silent as I appear. I'm not what they are expecting. There's some murmuring, shuffling in seats. I try to keep going. To lift my foot and put it down in front of the other, but I'm frozen. I can't move. I have no plan of how to start, or what to say. I look out at everyone. From the stage it looks like thousands of faces. Faces that are not even looking at me. Not interested in me. This is the *bad* version of the dream, and it's coming true.

There are people standing at the back, leaning against the wall. I see Mum and Chloe sitting up really straight. Mum has her speech therapy smile on. Chloe has her favourite pony on her knee. At the side I can see Dad; he gives me a thumbs up from behind the camera; he looks a bit confused when no one else comes on with me.

There's a little table on the stage with a glass of water on it. I'm holding the joke book so tightly that it digs into the tips of my fingers. I can see the little dents in the flesh where the edges have been. The blood rushing into them turning them from white to pink.

Everyone's waiting now. I see William Blakemore come through the double doors at the back of the hall. Ellie and her dad are a few rows from the front, smiling. I pick my leg up with my hands and move it in front and then the other one follows. I picture Mum's words and repeat them in my head: *Everything I say is important. Everything I say is important. Everything I say is important.*

When I eventually get to it, I tap the microphone. It hisses loudly. I clear my throat, open my book and begin, "H-H-H-H-H-H-H-H-H-H-H-H-H-H-H-H—"

Everything I say is important.

Giggling. One boy at the back shouts, "P-P-P-P-P-Pip!" Even more giggling. I see some kids at the back of the hall wrestling.

I stop and take a breath in, take a sip of water. *Everything I say is important. Everything I say is important.*

Then I try again, "H-H-H-H-H-H-H-H-H—"

I look out at all of the frowny/smiley faces staring back at me.

Then I look at Mum and see a sad smile on her face. I want to take that smile away for her. No, not for *her*. For *me*. I don't want anyone to look at me like that any more. Never again. I need to do something.

I close the book and put it on the little table. I take the microphone off the stand, pull up the chair and sit in it. I cross my legs and sit back in the chair. "I h-h-h-h-h-hope you h-h-h-h-have nowwwwhere else to be tooooday." It's quiet, you could hear a pin drop. They're listening. They are REALLY listening. "W-W-W-We could be here for some tiiiime."

I take another sip of water. The audience chuckle. I feel something change in this moment. I feel it and so do they.

As I look out at everyone, their faces and bodies look totally different. Relaxed. They aren't so scared any more. They're listening. The view has changed. They *want* me to talk now. They're interested. Even if I stammer. So I do.

"H-H-H-H-H-Hello, my name is B-B-B-Billy Plimpton and I h-h-have a s-s-s-s-stammer. I a-a-am meant to be up here with my baaand but they have d-d-d-ditched me." Another sip of water.

A few people say, "Ahhhh."

I carry on, "M-M-M-Maybe it was something I s-s-s-s-sstuttered."

Laughter. Proper laughter. It sounds amazing. Just like the laughter from the good version of the dream.

"When someone suggested I c-c-come up here and

tell some j-jokes I was speeeechless... L-L-L-Literally."

I see Skyla standing at the back with her mum. They are both laughing and wiping their eyes. I see Mr Osho put his hand on Mrs Able's shoulder. I'm enjoying myself now, enjoying the view.

"D-D-Did you hear the rumour about the butter? Well, I'm not about to start spreading it." I walk over to the drums and at the punchline take the sticks and play a huge *BA-DUM TSSSHHH*.

People whoop so I play a huge roll and drum solo.

"W-W-Why did the ch-chicken j-j-join a band? Because it already had s-s-s-some drumsticks." At this I pretend to be a drumming chicken, clucking and hitting the cymbal. People are loving it. I stand up and put the microphone back into the stand; I'm just thinking about how to finish. What to say. But I realize I don't want to stop. I want to say more.

So I go on.

"S-S-S-S-S-S-S-S-S-S-S-S-S-S-S-S-S-S S-S-S-S-S-S-S-S-S-S-School ... wow, that one was a big one, wasn't it?!" More laughter, more relief, I can feel people stop worrying about me. "Has n-n-not been easy f-f-f-for me. Buut I don't think it's easy for anyone, i-i-is it? Whether you want t-t-to beeee more n-n-normal or whether y-y-you s-s-s-struggle with m-m-m-maths."

I look at William Blakemore and smile, and he smiles back at me.

"We all h-h-h-have our s-s-struggles. Even if we don't admit it. The problem wiiith mine is that I can't h-h-hide it. Everyone can hear when I a-a-am s-s-s-s-s-struggling. Maybe it's not such a b-b-b-bad thing.

"Maybe it's not good t-t-t-to hide f-from th-th-things that scare us. I did not want to do th-th-this. T-Talk like this. N-N-Not at all. I wanted to hide away from it. W-Wait until I was a different person. Until I had got rid of my s-s-s-s-s-stammer. Buuut now I'm here, like this, it's not s-s-so bad. M-M-Maybe I'm OK as I am."

Someone cheers at this, and people begin clapping again. I look at Skyla and know what to do.

"We're all different. K-Kids, parents, teachers … especially t-t-t-teachers. Teachers are very 'different'. You know who I mean."

Then I launch into my impressions and the whole place goes crazy. Skyla is standing up and cheering throughout. I can see that some of the teachers are wondering if it's OK to let me carry on; should everyone be laughing at a science teacher falling asleep? But even they can't help but laugh when I'm scratching my tummy like Mr Randall and doing sums as fast as I can.

"Four times four is sixteen. Yeah, give me another, another. I love m-m-maths. Throw me a ball. I love maths more than b-b-balls. Fetch, sit, paw, roll over. I'm a good maths p-puppy. Pythagorean theorem, algebra, geometry." Then I start panting and roll on my back like I'm exhausted. A huge round of applause.

I know it's time to go, and as I stand up and pick up the microphone, I see my mum smiling up at me, I imagine the beautiful curly handwriting and I realize something.

"My m-m-m-m-mum always tells me that *everything* I say is important, but that can't be true, c-c-can it?" Mum looks confused now. "EVERYTHING?! That's a l-l-l-lot of responsibility, Muuuum!" More gentle laughter, Mum has got the red blotches on her neck but she's smiling. Listening. "How aboout this... Fart. P-Pants. Poo head, worms. That isn't *important*."

More laughter, Mr Osho is holding his stomach.

"It wasn't, was it? It was s-s-s-s-silly. Really silly." People are wiping their eyes and I don't know if they are laughing or crying. "P-P-P-Paris is the capital city of Ch-Ch-Ch-China. That's not important either. It's wrong! Sometimes I s-s-say things that are just plain wrong. We all do. Like when Mr Grant calls me

Bobby! I d-d-don't mind, Mr G-G-Grunt, honest!"

Mum is nodding now and has her hand over her mouth. I know she feels bad so I wink at her. "I can s-s-s-say things that are mean (which I do to my sister), th-thoughtless (to my friends), funny (hopefully now) and poetic. I c-c-c-can say something and change my mind in the very next moment. I can say sorry. So not *everything* I say is important and that's OK, isn't it? It is more than OK... It's great. I have already s-s-spoken f-f-for longer than anyone would have imagined. I c-c-can see that my m-mum is about to cry ... a lot! She h-h-has th-that look on her face. Thanks, everyone. Goodnight!"

I have never heard so much noise in the hall before. Everyone is on their feet and most of the mums look like they are crying. Even some of the dads. I stand there for ages not really knowing what I'm meant to do. So I look up to the ceiling and whisper, "I did it, Granny Bread, just like I promised." Then I take a big over-the-top bow and then put one foot in front of the other and leave the stage like a chicken playing the drums.

CHAPTER 31

**What was the snowman doing in the vegetable aisle at the supermarket?
Just picking his nose.**

After the show Mum and Dad won't stop hugging me, but I'm too happy to be embarrassed. When I lift my head out of Mum's tight grasp I see Ellie and her dad coming over. He looks a bit emotional and says, "I wish I had seen something like that when I was a kid. That was incredible!" And then he hugs me too!

Ellie just laughs and says, "I think you made a big impression! Well done, Billy. See you soon, eh?"

I watch them as they leave the hall, her red hair bouncing out of the door, and suddenly I feel completely exhausted. Exhausted but totally happy. When I notice tears rolling down my cheeks I finally understand why Mum sometimes cries happy tears. As I wipe my eyes I see Mr Osho heading over, not even trying to hide his tears. He gets to me and says, "Billy Plimpton, I have never been more moved or proud of another human being in my whole life. I bow down to you," and with that he gets on his knees and pretends to worship me.

"M-Maybe don't do that in class, sir," I say, smiling, and he stands up and gives me a huge hug.

When the news goes out on telly I kind of become a bit of a celebrity. They want me to go on and do an interview in the New Year! On the last day of school, some kids come over to our table in the dinner hall, they want me to sign their lunch bags! They keep calling me "a legend".

The Regulars are now officially back together. I much prefer jazz drumming to rock anyway. As we're taking all the instruments back into the Music Lounge from the theatre, Blakemore sees me struggling with a cymbal and takes it off me.

"Maybe I could be your roadie, Plimpton?"

"Yeah, or even b-better, The Regulars are looking for a lead singer? I bet you sing like an angel, Blakemore, don't you?"

"You better believe it, Plimpton," he says and then

launches into some loud opera, "Just one Cornetto, give it to me."

"You're in!" I laugh as we head into the Music Lounge.

Mr Osho is sitting at his desk and I look in my rucksack and take out my drumming notepad.

"Billy!" he says, smiling up at me.

"Sir, I th-thought of something to write," I say, handing over the book. He takes it from me and opens up the cover. Inside, is a long list covering every inch of space, and next to every number from 1-100, it says, *Thank you*, written over and over again.

"Billy Plimpton, I am not going to let you make me cry twice in one week. Now come here and give me a hug and then let's get out of this place until next year, shall we?"

A few days later I get a Christmas card from Sue and a note saying how proud she was when she saw me on the stage. Mum sent her a link to the news clip and Sue says that she's going to show it to all of her clients to "inspire" them.

On Christmas Eve, we're all sitting round the table playing cards. Me, Alex, Josh, Matthew and Skyla. Chloe's invited Aisha over and they're galloping around when Aisha points at the window and screams, "It's snowing!"

By the time we've finished playing the game there's a thin blanket of snow over the garden. As everyone's getting their coats on I run up to my room to get my snow trousers and an extra pair of socks. As I'm rummaging in the wardrobe I feel something hard in among all the coats. I bring it out and see the Nike tick. Granny Bread's box. I sit down on the bed and immediately forget about the snow. I carefully unravel the sellotape and look at all of the letters. I can't even remember why I'd hidden it from myself.

I smile and put the little bottle of shells on to my bedside table. I take one of the notes and pin it on my pinboard next to Scraggles. I lean the octopus card on my desk and then put the rest back in the box and under my bed. It feels comforting knowing it's there. That Granny Bread's still here.

So strange how something can feel scary one minute and not at all the next. I take one more look at the shells and then pull on my trousers and run down the stairs. We collect all of the snow off the car and make a stash of snowballs. Then Mum and Dad let us throw them at them, like they always do. Everyone looks so happy and I realize that even after everything that's happened I feel really lucky. Lucky to have my friends and my family all laughing around me.

Then I throw a perfect snowball and it hits Dad right on his neck and goes into his coat. "Ha! Take that!" I laugh.

"Right, Billy Plimpton, this is war!!!" he shouts as he launches a huge attack on us. We all end up lying in the snow laughing as Dad hurls snowballs at us. After that we all make Chloe a huge snow pony. So in a way she gets exactly what she asked Father Christmas for.

On Christmas Day I get exactly what I want too. A beautiful orange suitcase record player. It looks great. To go with it Dad bought me loads of vinyl. They got me some comedy and loads of music too. I didn't know that you could even listen to stand-up comedy on vinyl!

Here is the list of what I have:

1. Monty Python
2. Miles Davis
3. Morecambe and Wise
4. Arctic Monkeys
5. Ella Fitzgerald

6. Rowan Atkinson
7. Nirvana
8. Dizzie Gillespie

It feels really good listening to Miles Davis again. I look at all of the pictures on the record sleeve and read all the stories about the songs on the sheets inside. I love the feel of the records and their covers, they feel special. Important. I'm going to take good care of them and wipe them with a special cloth like Mr Osho showed us once.

When Granny Bread's favourite song comes on I reread all the notes from the Nike box and hold the little bottle of shells as I listen. I fall asleep and dream about Granny Bread swimming with an octopus. When I wake up and imagine Granny Bread wearing a snorkel, mask and flippers I get the giggles so bad that I can't stop.

CHAPTER 32

Not to brag but I have a date for New Year's Eve.
December 31st.

There are five minutes until the New Year. Mum and Dad are downstairs trying to stay awake until midnight. They think I'm asleep but I really wanted to stay awake.

I'm spending a lot of time in my room listening to music now. I bought some more records with my Christmas money. I LOVE record shops! I think Mum wishes they hadn't given me the record player. She says: "I never see you any more!"

After lunch today Mum and Dad said they had a surprise, which was a "little bit different". I had no idea what they were talking about and could not tell from their expressions what they were feeling either. They looked like kids. Nervous and excited. They handed me an envelope and told me to open it. Inside was a black-and-white picture that looked really weird and blurry, I didn't know what it was until I noticed some writing on the bottom left hand corner which said, *Baby Plimpton*. I looked up at them and they had their arms around each other and were grinning like crazy. "You're going to be a big brother again!"

I can hear them downstairs. Only two minutes to go. I think this year is going to be great.

Well, it won't *all* be great, obviously. That would be impossible, and not very interesting. We can't just be one thing, can we? It's not that simple, is it? I'm made up of lots of different bits and pieces. Good, bad and everything in between. It's all what makes me Billy Plimpton.

I can hear them counting down. Here is my final list of the year. A list of all the things that make ME ME.

"Ten!"	My name is Billy Plimpton and I am a comedian.
"Nine!"	I am a drummer.
"Eight!"	I am a big brother.
"Seven!"	I am a goalkeeper.
"Six!"	I am a grandson.
"Five!"	I am a public speaker.
"Four!"	I am a writer.
"Three!"	I am a friend.
"Two!"	I am amazing, incredible and unique.
"One!"	And I am normal.

Oh, yes, and I also have a stammer.

Happy New Year!

ACKNOWLEDGEMENTS

Knock knock.
Who's there?
Tank.
Tank who?
You're welcome.

Soon after I began writing this book (when I had no idea if it would ever be published), I became fascinated by acknowledgements pages. I found myself in bookshops flicking to the back of book after book, to read about who everyone was so grateful to, imagining their life and writing process. Now here I am writing my own!

Thank you to my wonderful agent, Chloe Seager; I will never forget getting your first email. The whole team at Madeleine Milburn really are the best; thanks to all of you for sending Billy's words far and wide.

Huge thanks to everyone at Scholastic (on both sides of the Atlantic), you have all shown me just how great "book people" are. Harriet, Pete, Jenny, Liam, Bec, Penelope and everyone else who I have not had the pleasure of chatting to directly – you are all brilliant at what you do.

Andrew Bannecker, thank you so much for the beautiful illustrations. My editors – Lauren Fortune and David Levithan – you are amazing. I can't thank you enough for all of your help in shaping this book.

To the lovely lot who read my early drafts and chatted through ideas, back when Billy wasn't even Billy. Nanny Soup, Granny Bean, Jools, Colette, Ben, Jen and Bridget. You gave me both feedback and hope. Thanks!

Finally, to my family who have cheered me on the whole way. Cleo, who listened to me read numerous different drafts over many many bedtimes, you are my shining star. If I ever find that real life unicorn – it's yours. Lenny – this story would not exist without you. I have learnt so much about life from how you live yours. You have not only been my inspiration but my mini proofreader, your hawk eye misses nothing! Rob, as your head is barely ever out of a book, it is only fitting that you are now mentioned in one. Thank you.